Samuel Barber

Beneath Helvellyn's Shade

Notes and sketches in the valley of Wythburn

Samuel Barber

Beneath Helvellyn's Shade
Notes and sketches in the valley of Wythburn

ISBN/EAN: 9783744743310

Printed in Europe, USA, Canada, Australia, Japan

Cover: Foto ©Andreas Hilbeck / pixelio.de

More available books at **www.hansebooks.com**

'BENEATH HELVELLYN'S SHADE.'

BENEATH
HELVELLYN'S SHADE.

NOTES AND SKETCHES
IN THE VALLEY OF WYTHBURN.

BY

SAMUEL BARBER,

AUTHOR OF 'THE LOST VILLAGE,' 'BALMORAL TOWERS,' ETC., ETC.

> ' How bountiful is Nature ! He shall find
> Who seeks not, and to him that hath not asked
> Large measure shall be dealt.'
> WORDSWORTH.

LONDON :
ELLIOT STOCK, 62, PATERNOSTER ROW.
1892.

PREFACE.

TOPOGRAPHY is a wide subject. If carried out in what is termed the scientific spirit, it is indeed absolutely boundless. To say nothing of geology or botany, a single pond, with its desmids, diatoms, polyzoa, water-mites and larvæ would afford material for a volume. A fragmentary or sketchy treatment seems thus to belong to this subject, if the area described be at all considerable.

Yet though the treatment may be partial, accuracy, and indeed thoroughness, need not be sacrificed. In the following pages the writer has endeavoured to be exact so far as it was possible, and he trusts the work may not be devoid of interest to Lake-land tourists and others, as well as natives of the Wythburn district. He takes this opportunity of thanking Professor

Ruskin for the use of part of a private letter, on the subject of clouds ; and also to Messrs. Allen for their kind permission to reprint the substance of two articles by the author, from the *Popular Science Review*. In a mountainous country the forms of cloud are almost always a prominent feature in the landscape, and considerable space has therefore been given to them. The author of the Book of Job, Homer, Wordsworth, Sir J. Herschell, Ruskin, all studied the clouds. The laws which relate the component molecules of a cloud to its general form, and those, again, which relate that mass-form to the earth by varying altitude, offer a most interesting field for research ; that there is great practical use in accurate knowledge of clouds, the present year, 1892, has abundantly shown, almost every thunderstorm having been preceded by one or more of the best known electrical forms.

With regard to antiquities in the North of England, it is gratifying to observe that, especially in the Furness district of Lancashire, considerable interest in parish customs, folklore, etc., is arising among the clergy. The result—a matter of vast importance—

will be an increase of historical knowledge among the people. This knowledge, dependent on the care with which the work of collecting and recording local facts is carried out, cannot fail to encourage social stability by developing patriotic feeling. Multiform are the lessons of the ' antiquary times.'

These Wythburn Sketches now commended to the reader's kind indulgence have been drawn up under difficulties, and with little assistance from books or personal sympathy. May they give to him as great a fund of amusement as they have afforded to the writer ; and if they haply chance upon the table of some sojourner upon the hills,

' Remote, unfriended, solitary,'

may they stimulate him to look carefully around his own dwelling-place, and go and do better.

The influence of a Sedgwick, a Henslow, or a Hugh Miller may kindle enthusiasm far and wide, and the stimulus of humbler examples will not be without its educative effect. The knowledge of history entailed by the study of antiquities, and the habit of reflection developed by examining the wondrous processes of nature, are matters of national concern. It would be

hard to imagine a more valuable boon bestowed on
our rising generation than the faculty of observing,
with brains as well as eyes, the marvels with which
the Divine Hand has encompassed us.

If this little work tends to enforce the acknowledg-
ment of an inspired naturalist, the writer will be abundantly satisfied :

> ' O Lord, how manifold are Thy works !
> In wisdom hast Thou made them all ;
> The earth is full of Thy riches.'

CONTENTS.

—◦—

CHAPTER I.

CHAPTER I.

THE VALLEY—THE CHURCH—NAVVIES—THE NAG'S
HEAD—CHRISTOPHER NORTH.

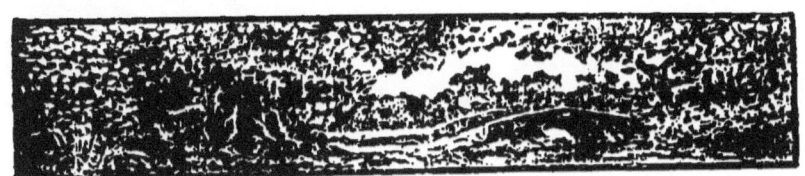

I.

LOOKING across the narrow, green valley of Wythburn, with its rushing brook and hedgerows dotted with sycamore, my eye falls upon the massive wall of Helvellyn, which, seen from the window at which I write, looks almost perpendicular. The numerous pedestrians (with a horse or two at times) ascending and descending the time-worn track that has done duty for 2,000 years, look like mere specks. A bright white moving spot generally indicates a young lady, a black and white one flitting to and fro, now behind and now in advance, her gentleman comrade. Upon the delicately curved sky-line of the mountain top beyond there move slowly along one, two, three dark little specks; these are the successful climbers who have just attained the object of their ambition, and are nearing the summit. Down the grassy slope by the ghyll at the foot of the mountain three gray objects rapidly descend in Indian file towards the high road that runs along its base; these are collegian tourists that have walked over from Patter-

dale, rejoicing in their escape from the anxieties of
the Senate House, and now making straight for the
Nag's Head. There they mean to do proper justice
to the 'tea and chops,' and to inscribe their names in
the much thumbed and motley collection of auto-
graphs that is always at hand to divert the impatient
traveller. How often will they talk over their day's
adventure on the mountain, and how much like a
dream will be the memory of it when a few short
years are past !

From the citadel whence I look down upon the
eager and ever-moving stream of the pleasure-seeking
world below, a path descends through seven fields,
crossing a brook by the way, to the well-known inn
where Wordsworth, Christopher North, and the Cole-
ridges met and cracked their jokes. Here is a coach-
ing-station between Grasmere and Keswick, and from
this point it is usual to ascend Helvellyn, on the
western side ; and here the tourist is invited to enter
and survey the little whitewashed church so fitly
characterized by the poet of Rydal Mount :

'Wythburn's modest house of prayer.' *

And truly, for a primitive little mountain church it
would be difficult to find a better. Neatly restored
and amply large enough for the wants of the people, it

* The building must have looked even more ' modest ' before
the erection of the little bell-tower by the Manchester Corporation.—S. B.

possesses a variety of interesting associations, and, chiefly through the writings of Wordsworth, is a great favourite with tourists. The chancel and circular arch are palpably enough of recent construction, and the stained window, though also new, is harmonious and artistic enough to gratify connoisseurs in art. This window is one of the few erected as a memorial during the life of the person memorized, viz., the Rev. B. R. Lawson, upwards of forty years vicar of the parish.

This church has obtained greater renown than usually falls to the lot even of notable churches, through its peculiar position, church and inn facing each other, and apparently forming a kind of joint concern ! The custom with travellers on arriving here from Grasmere or Keswick is to step from the coach-top to the summit of the wall encircling the churchyard, and then, after inspecting the building, proceed for refreshments to the Nag's Head. If there is a defect in Wythburn church it is want of light, and if this defect should ever be remedied it will doubtless be through the roof, this being the most economical method. An extra space of window is certainly required, through the overshadowing presence of the mountain.

At the present date, 1890, the evils arising from too close proximity of church and inn are aggravated, and that severely, by the insufficient accommodation for the colony of 'navvies' continually on the spot. Though the presence of these 'pioneers of civiliza-

tion' brings 'grist to the mill,' it cannot be pronounced altogether a blessing to a country inn of the
dimensions of the Nag's Head.   Much less is it one
to the children attending school or the worshippers at
the church.

At this ancient hostelry have gathered together
many notabilities both past and present—lake poets
and philosophers and dignitaries of Church and State
preparing to scale the brow of the ' Mighty Helvellyn,'
or to inspect the 'smallest church in the country,'
' the church where Adam and Eve were married,'
etc., etc. ; and, occasionally, if time permitted, to pass
the evening under that quaint old roof where Wordsworth, Wilson, De Quincey, and Coleridge must often
have met to indulge in high transcendental dialogue,
after tramping by ' fell and fountain sheen ' through
all the district round.

But all this was before the days of the invasion of
the M. C. W. Committee.   We wondered now and
then what Wordsworth would have said could he have
arisen from that peaceful corner in the churchyard of
Grasmere to behold the gambols and hear the
dialogue of our friends the navvies in and out of the
far-famed Nag's Head.   Equal, at least, would have
been his indignation to that which possessed his soul
when ejected from his pony-carriage by the impact of
a coach at the brook side in the valley below.   But
we venture also to assert that not with ' Punch ' and
' Billycock ' and ' Yorkey ' only would his wrath be

concerned. Rather, we suspect, would it be with the treatment that these much maligned pioneers have received at the hands of contractors and local authorities, and with the general neglect by 'Society,' which has left them almost entirely outside the pale of religion and civilization.

The ubiquitous tramp, representing the scum of the country, attaches himself, like a blood-sucking parasite, to the navvy, and thus the fraternity of 'excavators' is dragged down to lower depths, like the victims of the 'Old Man of the Sea.' Verily, 'Yorkey' and 'Punch' have need to pray for deliverance from their friends. I may say here that the life of these hut communities presents many interesting social problems. Unlooked for civility and much appreciation of kindness are often shown by these unfortunate wanderers.

Space, however, will not allow of details concerning the great 'Navvy Question.'

We conclude this chapter with an incident of a different order, relating to the Nag's Head, told by an old inhabitant to the present writer, and still a cherished piece of local lore.

Scene: The little parlour of the Nag's Head. Shades of night falling after a grand September day.

Present: Christopher North, De Quincey, S. T. Coleridge, and Lal Hartley.* Everything jovial. Day's adventures talked over and bedtime near.

---

* All the 'personæ' cannot be vouched for. —S. B.

Enter landlord after shooting on moors, with gun, loaded, which he places carefully in a corner.

By-and-by Christopher takes the gun and pretends to examine it. The company continue to philosophize, but eye the professor suspiciously. North quietly proceeds to the fireplace, and slipping the muzzle up the chimney, fires. Tableau—frightful noise, and avalanche of soot, in which the 'Lal' poet is completely enveloped. The company prepare to seize culprit, but he bursts off through the door upstairs, and bolts himself in. Great excitement, and Hartley is with difficulty cleansed from his mantle of soot.

Early next morning the professor is found to have vanished. It was a good while before he appeared again at Wythburn.

CHAPTER II.

CHANCELLOR FERGUSON'S HISTORY—DIALECT POETS — RICHARDSON — SHEEP-SHEARING — SHEPHERD'S SONG—FUNERAL CUSTOMS.

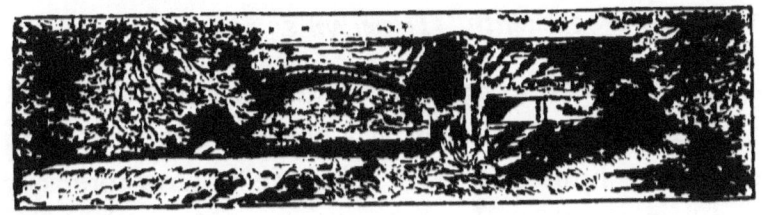

II.

CHANCELLOR FERGUSON, in his recently published popular 'History of Cumberland,' appends to his work a short list of local Cumbrian poets. The names noted are those of Relf, Clark, Anderson, and Sanderson. To these let us add Richardson.

In passing, it may be well to remark that brief accounts of local celebrities very fittingly find a place in a county history, and notably so those of dialect poets, whose writings so graphically depict the life and customs of their own country folk.

Richardson, who was schoolmaster at St. John's-in-the-Vale, is thus spoken of by the Rev. H. D. Rawnsley, in his 'Coach Drive at the Lakes': 'A man of racy shrewdness, and deep feeling for the realities of life; a man that Cumbrian literature will never forget; a genius St. John's Vale may be proud of.' It is quite true that the racy and realistic vernacular poet whose writing smacks of the soil is not often widely read. How many working men or tradesmen know anything of Barnes or Edwin Waugh outside of Dorset and Lancashire? Yet what a power are these men in their own limited area of influence! How intensely and how vividly their rustic pictures and their graphic portraits of individual character come home to the men of these two counties!

So has it been with Richardson over a more restricted area than that of Barnes or Waugh. In his case the strong bond of family associations, and the element of 'clan,' without doubt very strong in this district, have doubtless conduced largely to his influence. But his strong humanity and keen sense of humour have certainly given great force to his simple and touching songs of the affections. Among these we may cite 'The Blind Grandmother,' 'It's Nobbut Me' (a great favourite), 'Auld Scheul Friends'; these are characteristic of the homely spirit of his work. He also wrote some hunting songs which have been very popular.

Richardson was born at Naddle, near Keswick, in 1817, and died at St. John's-in-the-Vale in 1886. His widow and daughter were still living in 1890, and one of his nieces resided at Wythburn.

His copyrights were purchased by Mr. Coward, of Carlisle. There are, I believe, few, if any, unpublished poems of Richardson remaining.

Before he became schoolmaster at St. John's-in-the-Vale he was engaged in the building trade, and very creditable work of his is said still to exist in Keswick.

Mention of the native poetry of the district brings us to the prolific subject of folk-lore and social customs, popular superstitions and traditions. On each of these much might be said in almost any mountain district, by an ingenious writer. But I must not repeat what is simply generic. It will, I think, be more satisfactory to the reader if I simply give a few illustrations of local custom, just as they have come under my own notice, at the Wythburn end of Thirlmere.

First, then, we have the sheep-shearing, and the ' Merry Night ' that follows.

Sheep-shearing must always be a grand event in a place where the people live by their sheep.

The sheep support the people, and the dogs make this practicable. The work, hard enough as it is, would simply be impossible without the dogs. To narrate the various virtues of the collie in this place would be quite superfluous, but I may, in passing, note that they do not take any salary for their services. The work they do is simply marvellous, and they do not, if hard worked, live long. One wonders, therefore, at times, how it is that there is no ' Dog Feast ' established in Cumberland !

To sit the whole of a hot summer day with sheep after sheep on one's knee, plying the shears, is certainly not the easiest business in the world, nor yet the lightest, and that a ' Merry Night ' should ensue upon it appears inevitable. A good supper, and afterwards a good talk on the day's proceedings, then a song or

two by some benevolent amateur, and the evening
begins. The instrument, violin or melodeon, is
brought forth, and the fun commences in real earnest.
No doubt a brisk flirtation takes place here in many
meetings. Then the beer is brought forward, and
the ancient process of drinking the 'Shepherd's health '
follows.

This custom deserves the study of antiquaries.
Strictly observed, the master or chief shepherd ought
to be raised aloft, or 'chaired,' on this occasion, and
the guests should revolve about him, glass in hand ;
but this chairing is, I believe, now usually dispensed
with. The persistent way in which the song is re-
peated and the chorus shouted, or rather 'yelled,' is
very suggestive of the ancient and savage times from
which it is evidently derived. There is a palpable
tone of defiance in this chorus which at once
recalls to mind the ferocity of the Scandinavian in-
vaders, and the wine bowls formed from their victims'
skulls ! The song is as follows :—

> '*The shepherd's health—and it shall go round—*
> *And it shall go round—and it shall go round !*
> *The shepherd's health—and it shall go round !*
> *Heigh O ! Heigh O ! Heigh O !*
> *And he that doth this health deny,*
> *Before his face I him defy.*
> *He's fit for no good company.*
> *So let this health go round !*'

For an account of the circumstances under which

this health was drunk, the dancing round the 'Shepherd,' the chairing, etc., I must refer the reader to Richardson's humorous account in 'Stwories 'at Ganny uset to tell' (Chapter on 'Auld Fashint Clippins and sec like').

How far the scenery of Wythburn valley will be changed by the waterworks and extension of Thirlmere lake, a year or two will, no doubt, determine; but with regard to the social customs of the inhabitants, it does not seem probable that Manchester will have much influence in modernizing the native mind, when we reflect that the shepherd's song given above is still sung with great gusto and continual repetitions at sheep-clipping feasts. It is a true relic of the ancient days.

Funeral 'feasts' retain their hold in this district. It is not long since one was held a few days after the death of a child, at eleven o'clock on Sunday morning.* The funeral took place before the service in the afternoon.

A large number of relatives and many neighbours were 'bidden' to the feast. The congregation on this occasion was, I believe, one of the largest ever seen in the church. The custom, so common in Cumberland, of *men* attending funeral services *with their hats on*, is certainly yielding in this district to a more reverent observance.

* Eleven seems to be the usual hour for these gatherings.—S. B.

The interest that attaches to Wythburn in the present day consists, with many tourists, chiefly in its associations with the poet Wordsworth and other literary men resident in the vicinity about the beginning of this and the end of last century. I am not aware that anyone has hitherto attempted to write the natural history, or to describe fully the antiquities of the place. But every tourist seems to be posted up with regard to the 'Rock of Names,' upon which William Wordsworth and his friends are believed to have carved their initials. The new road (elevated many feet above the old coach-road) now being constructed by the Manchester Corporation is, it appears, to be honoured by having the pieces of rock containing these names inserted in its wall. The place from which the inscribed pieces of rock have been taken will either be brought by the raising of the water close to the lake or actually submerged. It will be a curious puzzle, I fear, to reconstruct the signatures.

We notice here the delight in personal associations prevalent among tourists. This love of anecdote and individual reminiscences would, doubtless, have a beneficial effect if it led to a true study of the noble works of such men as the poet of Rydal Mount. Perhaps, however, the greatest benefit now accruing is the interest added by these personal incidents to a summer holiday.

CHAPTER III.

ANTIQUITIES—ROMAN ROAD—CURIOUS ENCLOSURES
—THE CITY—ANCIENT STONE CIRCLE—STEADING
STONE—CELTIC BRIDGE.

III.

IN Chancellor Ferguson's recently printed popular 'History of Cumberland,' we do not find any account of a Roman road running through Wythburn from Grasmere to Keswick. That the Roman station at Ambleside was an important one will hardly be doubted. That there was another, perhaps of equal importance, at Castrigg, situated between Keswick and Grasmere, is also admitted. Let me note also that there have been various Roman remains unearthed at 'Pavement End,' Grasmere; so that the question as to a Roman road running through Wythburn amounts to this: were the camps at Castrigg and Ambleside connected? All probability leans to an affirmative answer. At the same time it is right to state here that some inhabitants of Keswick are sceptical as to the existence of Castrigg Camp, despite the strong evidence afforded by the name itself. In discussing the probabilities of this matter, let not the antiquary fail to note the extreme beauty of the scenery, and the so-called Druidical circle near at hand.

Relics of ancient work also exist here. An aged and intelligent resident of Wythburn has assured me that during the alteration of some farm buildings at a place bearing signs of great antiquity, called Stenock, the remains of an arch of flat bricks was found some thirty years ago, and believed by those who saw it to be the remains of a Roman oven. The road which skirts this building has been built with singular solidity. Many of the blocks forming the edge or basement wall of the road are about a ton in weight. Doubtless some of the larger boulders have occasionally been used almost *in situ*, but many others must have been collected or rolled down the fell-side to serve as a support for this mountain road. The road has been called by some a 'pack-horse road,' but why a road merely for this kind of conveyance should be built in so massive a style is difficult indeed to conceive. In one place between Stenock and Westhead Farm the boulders are built up five or six feet high for a space of forty or fifty feet. It is a noteworthy fact that this road is now (1890) being used by the heavy waggons of the Manchester Corporation contractors. It is much wider in some places than other, obviously for the purpose of allowing conveyances to wait and give passage. The amount of building contained in the portion lying between Westhead and Stenock should be carefully observed. After passing Stenock the road, in a most serpentine and un-Roman fashion, crosses the Greta twice and turns sharp to the left towards 'The City.'

This hamlet, called 'The City,' is situated upon the ancient way, a little before it begins to ascend the rocky ground lying between Wythburn and Armboth. It is a marvellously picturesque spot, and the old-world character of the dwellings greatly enhances its artistic charm. Let us hope that charm will not disappear with the extension of the lake.

The new road of the Manchester Corporation on the west of Thirlmere cuts across the ancient road just above the ruins of Stenock. It runs at the back of, and above the city, and will open up lovely views for tourists on the western side of Thirlmere.

Plainly, the earliest inhabitants of this district occupied the west side rather than the east, the remains of primitive and curiously built dwellings and other structures, of doubtful use, being far more numerous on this side of the lake than on the other. A casual visitor would be surprised to find that there were nineteen dwellings between Waterhead and Steel-End Farm (at the Grasmere end of Wythburn), exclusive of ruins. There are six or seven of these ruins between the city and Steel-End, and numerous others upon the sides of the fells west of Thirlmere. Mr. W. Wilson, a native of the district, now manager of the Keswick Hotel, speaks of the various supposed uses of these early structures, and evidently inclines to the belief that they are the remains of primitive dwellings.

'Knowing all about cutting and storing peat on the fell,' says he, 'I am certain from the situation in which we find them, that they cannot have been of any use to those who procured peats from the fell, and anyone who has had experience among sheep must know them to be utterly useless as sheepfolds.'

In the same pamphlet, viz., 'Thirlmere and its Associations,' he has drawn attention to the earthworks on 'Castle Crag,' near Shoulthwaite Ghyll, which he takes to have been a fortress of the early Celts, and to which they fled when attacked by superior numbers of the enemy.

Putting together all these indications of an early population, and bearing in mind the existence of two important camps, one at Ambleside and the other at Castrigg near Keswick, we conclude that some road connecting these camps must have run through Wythburn Valley, and we take this solidly built way to be that connecting road, because it is palpably the oldest road in the district, and passes by the earliest remains of the primitive occupants.

'Why,' it may be asked, 'did the Romans make this road along the fell-side instead of through the bottom?' The answer is plain. It is better and drier ground, and gave them much better command of the valley as they marched from station to station.

No doubt they would be glad to have a good view of their wily foes, who doubtless harassed their convoys severely as they traversed these dangerous solitudes.

Let us now return to the hamlet called 'The City,' or simply 'City.' It would be hard to find a nook in England more enveloped in the very atmosphere of remote antiquity.* The farm called ' May Green ' (now a navvies' lodging - house, and soon to be obliterated by the advance of the lake) is a capital illustration of this old-world style. When this house was erected little notice was taken of plumb-lines, and a floor was by no means of necessity a plane. The solid boulder, washed down from the hill or deposited by the ice of the glacial age, is imbedded and utilized in the wall, and chiselling is quite dispensed with to make it flush with the 'biggin' around. The kitchen is sunk some feet below the surrounding soil. Altogether the place is rather suggestive of an amusing device of the aborigines than of architecture. Here, I suppose, in early days the May-pole was erected, around which the village children danced when the Roman soldiers might be seen tramping along the fell, and long before the cross was erected at Crosthwaite or the Gospel preached at Penrith. How different must the garb of those children have

* Thirlmere will extend for a considerable area over Wyth-burn Valley when the waterworks are finished and the level raised.

been from that of the little ones now passing to
and from the village school! In more recent times
weaving was actively carried on in this valley, and
a stone upon the hill-side near Armboth marks the
spot where, to avoid infection, trade was done and
exchange made of the fruits of native industry.

The 'Web Stone' and the 'Steading Stone' are
two interesting memorials of the early days of Thirlmere life, and the latter especially connects us with
early customs and local laws. It appears to have
been customary to hold a court at this stone, and on
such occasions doubtless the ' pains and penalties of
Wythburn ' were strictly enforced.

The curious so-called 'Celtic' bridge that crossed
from Dale Head to Armboth has already gone ; ' May
Green,' with other dwellings of the ' City,' will doubtless follow it ere long; the ancient customs and
'laws ' will, I suppose, soon be forgotten, and the
very character of the scenery changed, perhaps never
to reappear, as now seen from the Cherry-Tree or the
old Post-Office.

The Rev. H. D. Rawnsley, in his 'Coach Drive at
the Lakes,' alludes to the Vikings and earthworks at
the 'City.' Whatever connection the Scandinavians
may have had with this picturesque little hamlet, I
venture here to draw the attention of antiquaries to
the remains of a rude *stone circle,** which I have little
doubt dates from a period long anterior to the Danish

* Only a portion of the circle now remains.

inroads. It is so situated that the tourist almost
inevitably misses it. On approaching the 'City' the
visitor should turn into the field in front of the
cottages on the right, which face the main. road
across the valley. Entering the field and passing
the cottages towards the lake, he will find a line of
boulders arranged in semicircular form and surrounding an abrupt rock which juts out from the grass
within the line of stones. This rock is much polished,
as geologists tell us, by glacial action. The whole
space within the semicircle of boulders has been
quite cleared of stones. On ascending the flat central
rock we find a cavity cut in rectangular form, about
a foot deep and two or more in length, and opening
out at the steep side of the rock where it faces Thirlmere.

This circle of boulders would plainly have been
valueless as a means of defence to anything within
the enclosure. It has no resemblance to the basement of a wall, and although many loose stones have
been gathered to fill up the interstices of the larger
ones, it seems perfectly clear that the circle of stones
was never built to any great elevation.

A few feet outside of this line, jutting out from it
into the boggy ground, is a short line of large flat
stones sunk in the earth, that apparently formed the
base of a wall; they run out from, but probably had
no connection with, the circle. The original condition
of this circle itself was probably similar to the Arab

circle at Heshbon, figured at page 330 of Captain Conder's work on 'Heth and Moab,' with a natural rock doing the work of a central 'dolmen.' What terrible sacrifices may have been offered on this stone, and what strange mysteries enacted in the dark times when human blood was thought to propitiate the so-called deities of heathendom! Let us hope that the very numerous menhirs, etc., of Syria and India and of primitive England do not all record the practice of such barbarities. We must, however, notice that in Cornwall and other hilly parts of the country, a neighbouring rock appears to have been used in connection with the religious rites practised at these ancient meeting-places. Curious incisions have on various occasions been found upon the rocks. It has also been remarked by travellers in Syria and Moab that dolmens nearly always occur in situations where there is an abundant supply of water. This is undoubtedly a confirmation of the view taken above of the remains at the 'City.' With 'Thorold's Mere' close by, a brook within about one hundred yards, and a ghyll that thunders down from the fells just behind, we have a truly typical scene for the celebration of those mysterious rites, whatever their nature, and by whomsoever they may have been enacted.

CHAPTER IV.

SCENIC EFFECTS—TRANSFORMATIONS—THE FLOODED FELLS—TWILIGHT GLOW—CHIME OF THE TORRENT —HELM WIND—CLOUD PILLARS—GLORY AT ARM-BOTH—CLOUD PROCESSION.

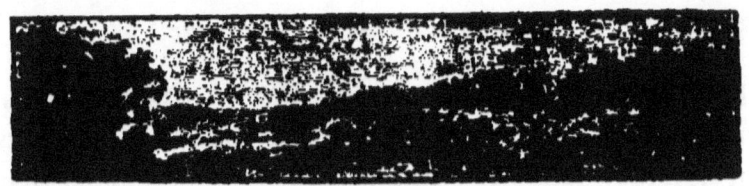

IV.

IT goes without saying that the strongest force of attraction to this, as to other remote mountain districts, consists in its 'scenic effects.' I am not speaking here of mere scenery, but of the transformation scenes of Nature's countenance, the flashes of the soul that breathes and the mind that gleams within and gives ever-changing 'expression' to her varied forms. The incessant change of feature arising from storm and sunshine, morning and evening, mist and shadow, gloom and brightness, and all their unlooked-for combinations, undoubtedly confers its consummate charm upon a landscape. The Londoner, fresh from the busy haunts of men, passing through such a valley as Wythburn, carries away a mental picture fraught with rosy hues and glorified conceptions, in which the subjective and objective find a happy union. In the sheep farmer, however, who climbs the bare hillside with his dogs a dozen times a day in pursuit of the means of subsistence, the subjective is often a *minus* quantity. 'Beauty lies in the eye of the beholder,' not only of the 'human face divine,' but of the aspects of nature. It is the striking and the phenomenal that is required to awaken the observation of the native, and cause *him* to dwell on the effects of scenery. The artist who tells you that his eye has become 'abused' by constant dwelling upon a certain series of objects is only repeating in another form what the fell-farmers mentally suffer from, viz., a need of the corrective influences of comparison.

It would be absurd to say that the face of Nature is at all times 'beautiful' (*i.e.*, to human perception), or that her beauty is not, at exceptional seasons, transcendently and abnormally so; and this certainly applies with emphasis to a wild mountainous district like that of Wythburn. The landscape here, like the weather, varies to a marvellous extent.

Among the more remarkable of what I have termed 'scenic effects,' the following may be noted as occurring during about a year's residence at this place; for, let it be noted, in relating phenomena of this class, that each season has its peculiar record, and that particular years may also abound in special features. Yet a lifetime will never exhaust the effects to be observed, and the oldest inhabitant, like the youngest, may readily meet with a glorious 'surprise,' so dependent are these transformations on the endless modifications of cloud and light.

The year 1890, in this district one of almost con-

tinual rain, was most rich in those effects that belong
to flood and fountain.

After a few days of unusually heavy rain a great
rush of water comes down by Dog Ghyll from Harrop
Tarn and the adjoining fells, and when the sun bursts
from the departing clouds a glorious sight is visible
from the coach road and valley near the 'Cherry
Tree' and Waterhead. In a short time this road will
be submerged, or at any rate disused. But this grand
sight will remain, and it is one of the finest to be seen
in the valley. Innumerable silvery streams, gleaming
in the sunshine, burst out upon the fell sides and
pursue their serpentine course down the mossy banks
and fern-clad slopes. Here and there a flat surface of
rock, coated by the descending stream, throws off a
dazzling sheet of brilliant light which resembles a
mirror in the full blaze of the sun. Numerous little
snake-like rivulets appear on the sides of the fell, and,
winding downwards for their appointed length, disappear again, like the rivers on the maps of Africa
that excited our wonder forty years ago. All is glitter-
ing with light, and the earth and air seem to vibrate
with the roar of innumerable torrents. The pure blue
sky and the bright green of budding fern and unfolding
sycamores constitute a delightful picture, that has
long made the 'City' and Wythburn Fells a lode-star
to the tourist's eye in spring and early summer. What
a contrast is all this to the dark and dreary prospect

from the western side of the valley on a drizzling
November evening ! Little does the tourist know
what it means to live in such a place as this the winter
through !

Next let us notice the view of Helvellyn from the
opposite side of the valley, when the ruddy light of
a winter sunset falls upon the snow that wraps in its
mantle the broad reaches of the mountain's breast.
It is nearly dark as we climb towards Harrop Tarn,
and the lights in the valley begin to glimmer un-
certainly in the mystery of the twilight. Yet the glow
remains on the upper pastures of the mountain and
reflects a weird, ruddy glamour to the valley beneath.
It seems to cling with strange pertinacity to the
heights, but dies slowly away when the stars begin
to peep out. I may notice also that a curious
luminosity about nightfall seems at times to shine
from the descending ghylls, especially when rushing
down after a flood. It would almost appear that the
water is affected by some kind of phosphorescence,
so strong does this glow appear at times. But this
remark can scarcely be applied to account for the
glow upon the heights.

We pause now to chronicle an experience of a
different order, viz., the natural music of the water-
falls. There is a passage expressing De Quincey's
delight in the river-music (quoted by Rawnsley in his

'Coach Drive at the Lakes'). It shows how the 'Opium-eater' and his friend Charles Lloyd listened to the Brathay waters' chime, and hearkened with profound emotion and awe to the sound of 'pealing anthems, as if streaming from the portals of some illimitable cathedral.' May we not say, indeed, that the entire expanse of the visible frame of Nature, ceiled with

' This glorious canopy of light and blue,'

is actually one grand cathedral?

Such 'pealing anthems' may be heard, though not at all times, issuing from the boulder-marked, steep declivities of Helvellyn Ghyll.

This music is best heard in the still air when the storm has departed, and a great mass of water is descending from the upper pastures.

To account for the harp-like sweeps of sound, the rhythmic cadences and deep bass undertones that strike at intervals upon the ear, we remember that the volume of music from the Ghyll itself is reflected from innumerable points and varying distances. This varied configuration, especially when the breeze is favourably responsive to the water's music, is probably a main cause of the natural orchestra, but not the only one. Doubtless it depends chiefly on the varying movement and mass of the descending water, and again, subjectively, on the sensibility of the hearer's ear.

3

'O marvellous music of the mountain pass !
O harper, that dost thrill the inner ear !
Can aught of mortal minstrelsy surpass
Thy voice Eolian, thine anthem clear,
Helvellyn Ghyll !　The wind of Autumn drear
With sudden burst about thy cataract raves,
Yet speaks with magic tones that waft me near
To sunny scenes beyond the rolling waves,
Where choral-girded sands a sapphire ocean laves.

'Music of Nature ! ocean wave and stream
Meandering mellifluous ; mountain rills
That chime sonorous, ray'd in silver gleam,—
Your pealing anthem the hushed spirit fills
With deep delight and awe profound, that thrills
Man's inmost being, for he heareth there
In sounding water, stream and echoing hills
And every movement of the ambient air
One master-touch supreme that tuneth everywhere.

'A touch that trembles on the shimmering sea,
That sways with organ swell where billows dash,
That whispers sweetly from the flower-strewn lea,
From every fell where floods as silver flash,
And where the mad cascades in fury clash.
Hark !　By the placid lake in slumber laid
A tiny tinkling tells the wavelet's plash !
Knowest thou whose hand their varied music made ?
Unheard, He heareth all, One is by all obeyed !

' "There is in souls a sympathy with sounds "—
So wrote a poet once, so all men feel ;
This universal frame o'erflows, abounds
With voices and with instruments ; a peal
Resounds, re-echoes, and soft harp-tones steal
Forth from the cataract that thunders strong
Upon the mountain steep : so thousands kneel
In some vast fane, a glad rejoicing throng,
And heaven receives their praise, accepts their choral song.'

S. B.

When the wind is about E. to E.N.E., *i.e.*, from the Ulleswater side of Helvellyn, and rises to about half a gale, a dry, brownish, smoke-like cloud settles on the top of the mountain, where it forms a kind of cap or 'helm.' Hence no doubt arises the term 'Helm Wind'; or, as it is often pronounced, 'Hellum Wind.' This wind and its attendant cloud have awakened a good deal of interest among observers of natural phenomena. The following remarks are rather suggestive than explanatory.

During my residence at Wythburn the cloud was seen chiefly in the spring. It is usually, I think, preceded by a few days' dry weather, and the wind is generally strong when it is seen fully developed. This last fact should be noted. The cloud has frequently the appearance of smoke rolling over the ground, and continually whirling about. The wind, even when blowing violently, does not disperse it. Its cohesion, and the tenacity with which it clings to the mountain, are most remarkable. The fringe of it hangs down over the fells, yet rarely divides. It is most unusual to see any portions pass across the valley.

This tenacity and affinity for the solid mountain are apparently due to some force of attraction.

The attraction is perhaps *only apparent*, and the following is probably a more rational explanation :—
The cloud is mainly a forming and dissolving one at the same time, and owes its origin to the impact of

a cold current on the invisible vapour rising from the ground.

The *dissolving* of the particles will thus take place chiefly at the edges of the mountain, where the cold wind meets warmer currents ascending from the valleys.

I have been informed that a very similar appearance is witnessed at Coniston, upon the 'Old Man,' and is generally attended there by a cold wind.

It is also strikingly manifested on Cross Fell, near Appleby. Such cloud phenomena present difficult problems. 'Who can tell the balancings of the clouds?' says the author of the Book of Job.

The 'Helm Wind' is generally gusty, and accompanied by a roaring noise and a whirling motion of the broken 'cumulus' clouds, which are evidently light in texture, and composed of small particles, though compact in form as they appear upon the mountain.

After rain, the formation of fresh clouds may be well seen on a calm day from the fell opposite to Helvellyn. The vapour rises in an invisible form to about two-thirds of the height of the mountain, and on reaching a certain elevation becomes at once visible, and ascends in well defined columns straight up in front of the rocks—pillars of ascending cloud, of which the base and lower part consist of *invisible vapour*. I may notice here, in passing, that clouds may be regarded as of two classes, viz., visible and invisible. The latter are often found among those that belong to the cirrus type, and which are consequently prismatic ; an illustration of which may be found in the *halo of fine cirrus* seen sometimes in a comparatively clear sky, and maintaining a circular outline due to refraction. The same may be seen when ice-clouds drift over the moon, as they pass into the position of a 60° angle of refraction.

The crimson glow on the crags is at times a glorious sight. It is seen most frequently in spring and autumn, and, at Wythburn, from the west side of the valley.

After a day's heavy rain, when the clouds roll away at sunset, and the streaming light of the setting luminary bursts beneath their retreating canopy, a deep crimson or ruby glow falls in a mass upon the top of the moss-clothed crags. As the rich red light gradu- ally fades away, first into deep-toned ruby and then into the sombre gray of dusk, while the giant peaks above assume weird resemblances and fantastic magnitude in the shadowy light, the hush of a deep peace seems to descend around us, and the landscape becomes, in the poet's phrase, ' most touching in its majesty.'

Descending to the point where the lake is narrowest, by the winding road which traverses the rough pastures known as Dale Head Park, we come to the bridge that crosses Thirlmere. Here the outline of the hills both near and distant is wonderfully varied. The

lake twists and winds with many a jutting rock and
inlet, sharp crags rising on one side and the lower
slopes of Helvellyn on the other.   The sunset effects
here are perhaps unrivalled in the district.   The
variety of outline in lake and hill, the pure and delicate
atmospheric tints, the gradation of light and shade
from the deep purple and gray of the sleeping lake to
the sunlit slopes of the upper fells, combine to produce
a picture which may well be termed 'The Artist's
Fairyland.'   But the tourist might stay for weeks, aye
months, before witnessing such a striking effect of
Nature's painting and of the Divine handiwork as the
writer saw one autumn evening in 1890.   Returning
from the west side of Thirlmere when the sun had
lately dipped behind the crags of Armboth, I was
traversing the lower road that winds through Dale
Head Park.   Deep undertones of green and gray,
purple and brown, wrapped the valley in a delicious
and softened harmony of colour, blending delightfully
with the evening stillness.   Brighter lights painted the
heights of the rocks and fells.   As I turned to survey
the track I had passed over, an exclamation of rapture
and delight burst spontaneously from my lips at the
sight that suddenly presented itself.   It was the
seventh heaven of colour.   An indescribably touching,
warm, and delicate tint of light gold had overspread
the whole of one slope of the mountain, softly spotted
and gemmed, as it were, by the boulders and crags
that marked its surface.   This light blended in tone

with the pure sky above, and contrasted most harmoniously with the stronger tints of brown and green in the dark woods and shadowy depths of the valley below.

Such a variety, richness, and harmony of colouring has, I think, rarely been seen, even here. 'Gloria in excelsis' is the involuntary response of the spirit when Nature presents such scenes to our view.

'The undevout astronomer is mad' has become a proverb, and it expresses in a word the spiritual teaching of Nature.

Might we not also say with the poet, on witnessing such scenes, that the undevout *mountaineer* is mad? Yet who will venture to assert that reverence is a noticeable feature of life in these remote valleys? I speak of the outward expression; for the inner spirit does exist, I think, among the people.

Once or twice in the early autumn there was seen from Westhead a striking cloud phenomenon. Advancing in compact line, and with almost level summits, a phalanx of grayish-blue cumuli descended with steady movement from the heights of Dunmail Raise, and solemnly pursued their way through the lower part of the valley towards the lake. Their upper surface was distinctly defined, and the objects on the slope of Helvellyn just above them were distinctly visible. This definition of the upper line in clouds of this character is unusual.

It is a fine sight to watch this continuous steady advance of the trailing cumulus clouds as they move through the calm autumnal air, drawn, as it appears, by some mysterious force of attraction to the other end of the valley. They rise over the pass, dip down quietly like a flock of gigantic sheep, descend into the vale beyond, and pursue their way as if animated by a common instinct. Doubtless there is a current of air running along the bottom of the valley, which bears them forward. Somewhat similar is the advance of a sea fog over the still water on a calm September afternoon, when the vanguard of the mist advances in well-defined packs towards the land.

On they come, not a breath of air moves, they ascend the hillocks and spread over the ground, the mist almost penetrates one's bones. Presently, the day disappears, and a vast impenetrable pall is spread over land and sea. In a few moments the whole of Nature's visage is transformed.

CHAPTER V.

V.

IT is believed by some geologists that many of the
lakes were, in former days, considerably larger
than they are at present, and that one main cause of
the lessening of their area has been the accumulation
in the valley of the detritus from the hills. How
many ages have elapsed since Helvellyn and similar
volcanic mountains stood in their full stature baffles
the imaginative to conceive. Like Dartmoor, I
suppose, they are to be reckoned but the stumps of
those fire-breathing giants that once poured their lava
streams over the surrounding country. And allowing
for change of climate, as indicated in a changing
fauna and flora, it is probably fair to assume that for
an immense period of time the same disintegrating
processes have been at work which are in operation at
the present day. Slow, but sure, is the mill that
grinds down the mountain range and pours its
particles into lake and sea. Prodigious, too, though
scarcely noticed, is the result of the working of those

'little things,' moss and fern, frost and raindrop, that effect this mighty transformation throughout the ages.

An interesting illustration of the power of these tiny workers is now to be seen on the side of the hill just above the old toll-bar on the Grasmere side of Wythburn Vicarage. There, imbedded in the green grass, close to the track of an old pack-horse road, lies a large boulder, whose descent from the jutting rock of Helvellyn above is a matter of recent history. About two years ago a party of men were playing a social game in the old toll-gate cottage, when a rumbling noise like thunder was heard for a few moments, and then it ceased suddenly and all was still again. In the morning the boulder, which had fallen from the cliff almost immediately behind, was found tilted on its edge in the grass above the cottage. It weighs many tons.

It was thought desirable by the natives to fix this erratic monster by digging an enlarged bed into which it might settle down comfortably and abstain from further careering into the valley. It would, indeed, have resulted in total ruin to the building if this stone had continued its descent, for the track, still visible on the hillside, shows that it was making for the cottage.

Not far from this stone, reposing in the field beneath, are two or three gigantic blocks, which, reasoning from the above incident, have probably fallen in the same way. Just above Stenock buildings are others still larger.

Another case of the descent of a boulder from the cliff on the side of Helvellyn took place on the 26th or 27th of January, 1891. The stone was about a ton in weight, and in its descent crossed the high road a few hundred yards on the Grasmere side of Wythburn Old Toll Bar. To the pedestrian or vehicle which had chanced to meet this headlong monster dashing into the valley it would have proved as 'awkward' as the railway train to the historic 'coo' which George Stephenson regarded with such composure. It crashed through the two walls on each side of the road, leaving a clear gap in each, and settled upon the lower pasture not far from the coach road, and the writer drove past not many hours afterwards.

Thus two notable boulders have transferred their resting-place from mountain to valley within a space of eighteen months. But I would ask the reader to reflect, first, how many such cases have happened without any record being made; and, further, what must be the sum of those which have descended in the vast periods of time which geology assigns to the epochs that have elapsed since the Cumbrian volcanoes arose, when storm and frost first began to batter their rugged sides? The enormous number of such stones now concealed *beneath* the soil may offer some reply to this.

The 'perching' of boulders by the agency of ice in the glacial period is now a generally accepted theory, and has doubtless been much corroborated by existing phenomena and processes still in operation. Still, such specimens as the 'Bowder stone' and the various large 'rocking stones' must remain a marvel on account of their magnitude. But when we reflect upon the immense periods during which the denuding processes now acting have been in operation, we should, I think, allow that a vast number of these mammoth blocks must have fallen during these long stretches of time, an inference corroborated by an examination of the deposit in the valleys. At Wythburn the process of making the new road on the west side of the valley has shown a large number of stones, probably so deposited, and containing volcanic ash, dark-gray granitic blocks, masses with undulating cleavage, spar with lead ore, etc., much of this being imbedded in red or ferruginous earth, also washed from above. The mass of gravel of this kind is, in parts, very thick, and the size of the stones varies from that of a pin-head to a boulder of 50 to 100 tons. The extent to which the smoothing operation of ice and snow has polished the rocks about Stenock and Dog Ghyll suggests again the extended duration of this age of the earth's history.

Certainly this valley affords an instructive lesson in the work of denuding forces; work which, unobtrusive and unregistered in man's history, has moulded, in ages past, the landscape of the present, and to-day is forming the landscape of the future. The effect of these forces in the production of soil, too, is a matter of such vital interest to the human race, and is here so strikingly brought before us, that we are led to consider the forces whose operation justly entitles them to be called soilmakers.

Next to the powerful and more mechanical effect of the forces above referred to, viz., ice and snow, wind and weather, we give the chief place to plants.

Yet the work of plants in disintegrating the rock is not only in the absorptive power and molecular forces that reside in the rootlets, pedicles, and the like, but may be seen sometimes exerting a powerful mechanical action in raising and splitting large blocks of stone from the foundation they have occupied for ages.

Not long ago I was standing in one of those delightful winding rocky lanes, partly formed by Nature and partly hewn by hand, which abound in Cornwall, when a builder, who was picking out the foundation of a workshop, pointed out to me the root of a fir-tree which had penetrated down into the solid slate rock from the high bank above, a distance of something like 20 to 25 feet. The thick root stem emerged from a chink in the freshly-hewn stone, and had the strong aroma of the fir upon it. These roots, piercing to so remarkable a depth, utilize those curious deep fissures which here often contain a deposit of marble, and which probably originated *after* the formation of the rock, when cooling from the intense heat of some volcanic upheaval.

Even fungus exerts, at times, strong mechanical action. It has been known to raise up and utterly displace heavy slabs of stone in a footway. The action, too, of small cryptogams, lichens, etc., is not a slight action in the end. If their work is slow, it is complete. The larger blocks of slate in some Cornish hedges are garmented with a continuous, close-fitting white lichen, whose growth defies calculation as to age, for it is continually rising, Phœnix-like, and spreading from its own ruins.

Large blocks of slate clothed with this plant are often as white as if covered with plaster, and I do not doubt that the lichen is sometimes as old as the towering sycamore that waves above it. Near the old town of Padstow, where lichens, together with hart's-tongue and other ferns, abound, the old slate hedges are often beautifully variegated, and their harmonious tints, in the later autumn, somewhat compensate for the absence of colour in the landscape around. Such a hedge-bank is pictured before me as I write; the fresh young tufted hart's-tongue peeping through the chinks of gray slate that compose the 'hedge'; lichen and moss covering the stone; the deep blue water of Padstow Harbour lying below, with the white sands of Rock and St. Enodoc glistening in the sunshine beyond.

How silently and harmoniously do the disintegrating

forces of Nature's tiny agents work! How mighty is their power! 'Gutta cavat lapidem, non vi, sed sæpe cadendo.'

Thus we see that a great variety of agents, some mighty and instantaneous in action, such as the earthquake and the hurricane; others slow and continuous for ages; some animal, some vegetable, some mechanical, some molecular, have for ages been at work in the production of that apparently shapeless substance which we term 'soil.' Did I say shapeless? An application of the microscope would for ever dispel that idea, for it would reveal organisms manifold, and minerals whose crystalline forms evidence the Divine hand of Him Who fashioneth all these things, as plainly as when He paints the lily or constructs the eye of the bee. But whether we regard the soil as a shapeless mass, or as 'architecture in disguise,' it is plain from the illustrations which have been adduced that it is a resultant product of forces infinitely varied, both in character, power, and manner of operation. To analyse fully, to catalogue and to expound the method of their operation would require at least a volume. Let us now pass on to the feathered inhabitants of the valley.

To enter at any length into the natural history of Wythburn would be beyond the purpose of these pages, so I shall almost confine myself to birds on the one hand and 'Vaporology,' as Professor

Ruskin has termed the study of clouds, upon the other.

The buzzard, the heron, and the wild duck are the most noticeable of the feathered inhabitants. The first-mentioned bird is frequently to be seen about the crags at the back of Westhead, and soaring over the fields on the western side of the valley. This hawk may readily be discriminated from the other species by the great breadth of its wings, which seem to cover almost all the space between the head and tail; and also by its circling flight. During the summer these birds depart to the high fells, where they spend the season. They were frequently visible in the spring of 1890, but not a single bird was seen by the writer during the summer. No doubt they had departed to more inaccessible places to bring up their young.

Walking one day between Westhead and Stenock, a wild duck rose up almost from my feet, soared over the wall, and skimmed away into the valley. A numerous progeny of yellow ducklings rushed about, piping with dismay. They divided into two companies, one of which made for a hole in the wall, into which they thrust themselves precipitately, quite regardless of the means of exit. The nest of this bird was probably placed on the mossy ground among the large boulders just below the road.

The heron, popularly termed a 'crane,' has usually been seen by the writer sailing over from Harrop Tarn down by Dog Ghyll to the low fields at the southern end of Thirlmere, or returning the same way. How leisurely and with what an easy swing does this stately bird move his pinions! Yet, when timed, it is found that they vibrate at least twice in a second. How different from the rapid whirr of the wild duck, whose wings vibrate at double or treble that speed! The flight of birds has been much studied of late years, and there are few more interesting subjects for the naturalist. Much more amazing, however, is the propelling mechanism of the bee, by which the tiny creature can keep pace with and at times even outstrip a carrier pigeon!

The raven is not common now in this district, perhaps never has been, its predatory habits being too well known to allow it to pass unmolested. The sheep farmers tell us that a raven or two can 'manage a lamb.' The name 'Raven Crag,' by St. John's-in-the-Vale, seems to indicate that these birds were more numerous before the days of fire-arms.

The kestrel I have not seen nearly as often about Wythburn as in the level country. On one occasion, however, I witnessed an aerial tournament between one of these birds and a buzzard. They dashed at each other repeatedly with no serious result. The buzzard made the most determined attempts to clutch his assailant, who easily evaded the contest, and returned, loudly shrieking, to harass his enemy. After this had gone on for some time, with loud cries on both sides, the kestrel skimmed away to a little distance, and began quietly 'wind-hovering' for his prey.

The cuckoo abounds in spring amid the fern-clad knolls and crags of Wythburn fells. One reason for this abundance may be found in the number of small birds whose nests are easily accessible, and whose movements can be watched from the rocks, in the nesting season. Those of the various chats, titlarks, wagtails, and the like, are doubtless found with greater ease in this open ground than in a wooded country, and the troublesome egg accordingly soon disposed of. Often may you see the sly old bird sitting upon a boulder or a jutting mass of rock, doubtless to survey the ground below, and mark the nesting-places of her would-be dupes.

Of all the smaller birds inhabiting this valley the stone-chat appears in spring the most numerous. Probably it does not greatly exceed in numbers several other species, e.g., the wren and the chaffinch, but its restless habits and its white patched tail-coverts render it more conspicuous.

Before the ferns and flowers are fully out, it is perhaps the most cheerful object that catches the eye of a strolling naturalist on these bare and rocky hill-sides. Its lively movements and chirpy trilling note render it an adornment to the solitude, and a slight compensation for the absence of those delightful summer visitants, the blackcap and the garden-warbler, which frequent our groves and gardens.

The summer in this valley seems so short that one wonders that birds of passage make their way here at all.

Of 'summer warblers' I may notice, however, that the willow wren is common enough, and may be heard among the larches as high up as Westhead. The garden-warbler and blackcap appear conspicuous *by their absence.* No wonder, when the size of the gardens attached to the various farms is considered. Surely there is room for more fruit-trees here !

The sedge-warbler is to be found along the brook by the 'City.' This bird has a wide range of habitat in England, and appears very common in Lancashire. It is a most amusing creature. One wonders at the exactness of the imitative notes, considering the *rapidity* of their utterance.

The tree-pipit and whin-chat are both found here, the latter being common.

Of hirundines the swift is but rarely seen. The house-martins, much less numerous than the swallows in many parts of England, are more numerous at Wyth-burn, almost every farm and cottage being tenanted by this home favourite. Sand-martins are somewhat rare, doubtless for want of sandy banks and soft cliffs wherein to burrow.

The thrush appears to be a commoner bird than the blackbird in this valley; at any rate it was so during the very wet summer of 1890. A few years ago the latter bird seemed in many parts largely in excess of the thrush, but, happily, the balance seems now restored.

With this note I will conclude my brief sketch of the ornithological features of the valley of Wythburn, which may, from the position in which it has been written, be termed a 'bird's-eye view' of my feathered friends.

CHAPTER VI.

PARSONS OF THE DALE AND MOUNTAIN—WALKER OF
SEATHWAITE—DOGS AND SHEEP—PET SHEEP.

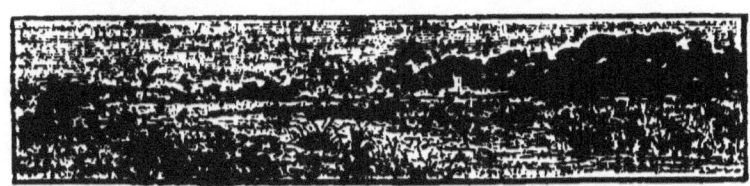

VI.

MUCH has been written concerning Cumbrian dalesmen—now, we are told, rapidly becoming extinct. But the characteristics of this hardy race, continually fortified by contest with a boisterous climate and social isolation, will be hard to obliterate. Certainly they have not gone from the district of Wythburn. The new order, indeed, has greatly encroached upon the old in the matter of homely occupations, such as spinning, candle-making, and the like, but this new condition of things is regarded habitually from the old standpoints. *We* are 'Cummerland fwoak,' and *you* are strangers, is an abiding truth, ever potent within the real dalesman's breast. 'We are the people of the place, and you are the midges which flit about us the summer through, for your own pleasure,' is his normal and constant feeling towards the world-stream that fine weather brings to his doors.

If, however, we cannot admit that the sons of the soil are disappearing very rapidly, so far as social customs go, it is doubtless true that the aboriginal 'parson of the dale' has now become a veritable 'antique.' The wonderful Walker type of parson may be considered about as extinct as the Dodo.

An antiquary may find, however, some attractive and amusing lore relating to the last vestiges of the race of 'dale parsons.' They were, like most other human beings, greatly the 'creatures of circumstance.' Anyone who has spent, like the writer of these pages, a severe winter in the vale of Wythburn, will understand that, though you may open your church, light a good fire, and ring a bell, you cannot compel the inhabitants to come to a service. Stories not wanting in authenticity are rife, which tell how, when the all-important business of publishing 'banns' has been committed to the vicar, it has been necessary to proceed to the village inn to beg some of the household to attend for this special purpose, long after service-time had passed ; and how, on another occasion, parson and clerk had to proceed, in an adjoining valley, to a farm at a distance for some witnesses to the legal declaration. One service on Sunday and none in the week (nor any other meetings), and congregations so reduced by bad weather as to be almost 'nil,' cannot be thought a condition favourable to developing clerical enthusiasm.

It is, perhaps, astonishing that men thus situated should in so many cases have contrived entirely to abstain from any practical devotion to art, science, or literature ; yet it will, I believe, be found that among

those so isolated only a small minority have dis-
tinguished themselves in such pursuits.

> '. . . Unless above himself
> He can erect himself, how poor a thing is man !'

is a truth that applies to a man's surroundings as well
as to his individuality.

Who can estimate the stimulating power of
sympathy ? Most of us have felt at times how much
the force of genial companionship and the friendly
rivalry of school days has had to do with our educa-
tion ; they have been powerful factors in our development, largely determining the after career, and
affording a stimulus more constant and more subtle
in operation than magisterial exhortation or the
golden glitter of a prize. In all these things, as
says the poet, most truly the boy is 'father of the
man.'

Much allowance is due to the eccentricities or
moral peccadilloes of a 'dale parson' or mountain
'priest.'* To a student of Nature the scenery of
mountain and moorland is a powerful incentive to
thought and research, and the classic adage, 'Nunquam
minus solus quam quum solus,' represents an enjoy-
able fact. But to those not gifted with a strong
desire to utilize leisure and to realize the charms of
that freedom which the old poet tells us is 'a noble

---

* This is the word usually applied to the church clergyman
by the people in many Cumberland parishes.

thing,' there is much of the oppressive and monotonous in remote situations. Too many among us need still to apply the Wordsworthian precept, 'Let Nature be your teacher.' 'Let no man,' said the philosopher to those who desired admission to the sanctum of his science, 'let no man who is not a geometer enter here,' and it might perhaps be for the happiness of some country parsons if the patron of the living inscribed upon the rectory gate, 'Let no parson who is not a naturalist enter here.'

The lowering effect of isolation and depressing weather, with a leaden pall of nimbus and a downpour almost unbroken for weeks together, causes some men to feel life hardly 'worth living.' Oh ! the blessed result of a real *living* hobby ; one which not only engrosses a man's faculties, but brings him into vital contact with the throbbing heart of humanity ! Thanks, ten thousand times to the penny and the parcel post which thus became the means of saving many denizens of the wilderness from the miseries of a morbid self-consciousness or a fixed idea.*

Good postal arrangements bring the life of the world, for the reader and thinker, to the most remote parishes, and perhaps the most valuable result to be obtained by this modern machinery is that it places

---

* During the month of August, 1891, the rain-fall in Borrow-dale was seven times that of some parts of England, and averaged nearly one inch a day. On *one* day it appears that as much rain fell as during the whole month at Boston in Lincolnshire.

the investigator of Nature or the litterateur *en rapport* with those that are of kindred tastes.

A number of Cumbrian clergy once discussed together what pursuit would be adopted by each as an intellectual refuge in case an isolated mountain parish were assigned to him. One spoke in favour of Geology, another of Art, another Natural History, and so on. At last a quiet individual was asked what hobby he would adopt. He promptly and decidedly replied, 'I should drink!' Sad, but perhaps not true alone of the candid one who made the remark. And the anecdote suggests a serious reflection for all who contemplate embracing a life of solitude, whether they have a sufficiency of spiritual and mental armour to fit them for the encounter with the enemy in the wilderness.

The custom of collecting 'Chapel Wage'—a toll generally amounting to a few shillings, from the fell farms, which exists also in the Furness district—is in some places, I imagine, in lieu of hospitality to the mission priest, who in former days took up his quarters in rotation at the various houses. It would appear that the clergy a few centuries ago did not suffer from an abnormally active brain, as the custom was to leave the sermons in church from Sunday to Sunday and draw them forth to be read as occasion required. So we can well believe that the priests of those days, some of whom could not indite a decent letter in English, were but little in need of *intellectual*

hobbies to divert their vacant hours. But the old
order has quite given place to the new. If the priest
of those days had to spend much of his time at the
fell-side farms, it would not be surprising that he
should assimilate largely to the style of the farmers
themselves, from whom he was often only one degree,
if at all, removed in birth and early association, and
not seldom came from their own class. Great was
the difficulty of obtaining well educated men to
settle in these lonely parishes. Can we blame the
bishops for stretching a point and ordaining men
who at any rate might sympathize with the farmer's
trials if they could not greatly elevate his mental
tone? The 'modus vivendi' was first to be found.

As bearing on the matter of a 'clergy supply' the
reader will find a letter addressed by Wonderful
Walker to the archbishop respecting the ordination
of his son, in the Notes to Moxon's Edition of
Wordsworth's Poems (1845). The account of Wonderful Walker is, indeed, wonderful enough; and in
spite of his long continued toils, clerical, scholastic,
and farming, he reached the age of ninety-three.

'In memory of the Reverend Robert Walker, who died the
25th of June, 1802, in the 93rd year of his age and 67th of his
curacy at Seathwaite.

'Also of Anne, his wife, who died the 28th of January, in the
93rd year of her age.'

Such is the inscription in Seathwaite churchyard
upon Walker's tomb. It testifies to the fact that he

at any rate needed not the reproof contained in the poet's lines :

‘ Withdraw yourself from ways
That run not parallel with Nature's course,’

for his habits must have been singularly in accord with the soundest principles of hygiene. His industry was certainly admirable. ‘Eight hours in each day during five days in the week, and half of Saturday, except when the labours of husbandry were urgent, he was occupied in teaching.’

But what would the High Churchman of to-day think of his manner of prosecuting his labours? ‘ His seat was within the rails of the altar ; the communion table was his desk, and like Shenstone's schoolmistress, the master employed himself at the spinning-wheel while the children were repeating their lessons by his side.’

Now comes the explanation of the mystery of Walker's leaving behind him a sum in thousands after holding a benefice of £35 per annum. ‘Nor was his industry with the pen, when occasion called for it, less eager. Entrusted with extensive management of public and private affairs, he acted in his rustic neighbourhood as scrivener, writing out petitions, deeds of conveyance, wills, covenants, etc., with pecuniary gain to himself and to the great benefit of his employers. These labours (at all times considerable) at one period of the year, viz., between

Christmas and Candlemas, when money transactions
are settled in this country, were often so intense that
he passed great part of the night, and sometimes
whole nights, at his desk.   His garden also was
tilled by his own hand; he had a right of pasturage
upon the mountains for a few sheep and a couple
of cows which required his attendance; with this
pastoral occupation he joined the labours of husbandry on a small scale, renting two or three acres
in addition to his own less than one acre of glebe,
and the humblest drudgery which the cultivation of
these fields required was performed by himself.'

But the frugality practised in Walker's household
was perhaps more remarkable than the industry which
he showed. 'The fuel of the house, like that of
their neighbours, consisted of peat procured from the
mosses by their own labour.   The lights by which
in the winter evenings their work was performed
were of their own manufacture.*   They are made of
rushes dipped in any unctuous substance which the
house affords.   'White' candles, as tallow candles
are here called, were reserved to honour the Christmas
festivals, and were perhaps produced upon no other
occasions.   Once a month, during the proper season,
a sheep was drawn from their small mountain flock
and killed for the use of the family, and a cow,

---

* The only approach to modern luxury that Wordsworth could
note at Seathwaite was the neat woollen covering of his 'family
pew,' spun by Walker's own hands.

towards the close of the year, was salted and dried for winter provision ; the hide was tanned to furnish their shoes.'

The picture is truly idyllic, and amid these multi-farious labours the noblest feature is that this mountain priest never lost his spirituality nor forfeited the dignity of his position. He was not only 'facile princeps' but with no second. Yet the thoughtful reader who knows this north country will recognise that Walker possessed enormous advantages over many of his modern brethren. He was supported by sympathy, for he lived among his own people ; he enjoyed the mental stimulus of living in a glorious country ; he was eminently adapted through his love of Nature to the position assigned to him by Pro-vidence ; he was, in fact, a born and accomplished naturalist, and last, but not least, the freedom with which he pursued his toils, and the interest which he took in them, were enhanced by the knowledge that his returns would be proportionate to his skill and industry. He led a free life and practically suffered from no 'clerical disabilities.'

How different the life of many a curate to-day ! Existing upon a pittance stipend, with no long-service pension in prospect, and all chances of preferment against him ; knowing that thousands more men are ordained than those for whom a 'living' can be pro-vided; preaching often to men of wealth, who care not to ask if he can meet his expenses, and who will not even give a guinea to the only society existing to augment his income; with all the yearning aspirations of spiritual life, and a burning desire for intellectual expansion, yet unable to purchase even books to continue his studies; for such men to continue toiling in towns through the best years of their life for the eternal interests of a cynical society, is in the writer's judgment a sight even more wonderful than the personality of a Wonderful Walker!

Only once in about a year's residence among the sheep-farms did a collie run at the writer with signs of ferocity. He was startled by suddenly catching sight of a stranger turning a corner. These dogs behave, as a rule, uncommonly well to strangers. There was a strong and nobly-formed creature that used to lie on the low wall in front of my room with steadfast gaze fixed upon the valley below, and ears intently listening to every sound that came up the hill-side. He had lost one eye by the onslaught of a cat. These country cats, I may note, are often more than a match for a dog. How I wished for an artist to paint that scene! Beyond, the mighty mountain, with soft, fleecy clouds hanging half-way up its steep green sides; above these the upper reaches of receding moorland, the tiny little white church slumbering at its base, the cluster of dwellings beside it, the deep stillness just broken by the chime of the waters and the merry laughter of the children just loosed from school, and the noble collie with limbs extended upon the low wall peacefully watching the scene below. But let the master's call or whistle be heard, and in a moment he is down and across the fields, scouring the stray sheep away to their proper feeding-ground. A truly typical Cumbrian picture.

Out of five of the farm dogs, two occasionally attended my walks. One of these possessed some *clerical* sympathies, and not only continued with me in a long visiting round, but once, when I had taken a mission service among the navvies then working in the valley, came and stood quietly by my side upon the platform, facing the audience as I addressed them. It was dangerous to attempt a removal.

Not a little has been written on the independent powers of some dogs in taking sheep from station to station. The story, however, of the collie that would take a flock without a shepherd from Ambleside to Keswick, stopping the would-be wanderers at every lane and 'lonnin,' usually excited a significant smile upon the faces of Wythburn farmers. This tale was just a little too strong for them.

In good faith, however, we were told of sheep being so taken home by a dog, from Cockermouth Market to their owner's place a mile or two away.

The instances of sheep returning from long distances to their early home pastures, traversing a town on the way and often doing the journey by night, are very curious and well authenticated. The shepherds

5—2

meetings upon the uplands of Skiddaw and Helvellyn
to restore and receive again their long lost 'woollies,'
the jovial good feeling that presides on these occasions,
the invigorating climb up the hill-sides, the tales that
beguile the way, the lively clamour of the gathering,
and the enthusiasm and splendid work of the dogs, all
combine to form a striking scene, and one that abides
long in the memory of those that witness it. For a
lively and full description of this episode of Cumbrian
life I must refer the reader to the animated description
of the Rev. H. D. Rawnsley, of Keswick.*

When the hounds are in full cry along the mountain-
side, the echoes of their music from rock to rock round
this close-pent valley strike somewhat strangely upon
the ear, and as you watch from the fell-side opposite,
the sound rises and falls and comes wafted close to
you, but you rarely catch sight of the dogs. Marvellous, indeed, does it seem that a hare can be
tracked at all over such ground and at such a pace;
but this is quite a favourite hunting-ground for the
Windermere harriers. A notable pack is that long
kept by Colonel Ridehalgh, of Fell Foot, and many a
day of keen sport have they given to the gentry of the
district. Up and down the mountain-side twice or
even three times in a day, after a journey by boat and
carriage from the far end of Windermere, with perhaps
a five or six mile walk thrown in, seems a pretty good
day's work.

* See *Cornhill Magazine*, 1890.

The singular force of the faculty of scent possessed by these hounds was amusingly illustrated in the case of a young member of the pack which lodged at the farm where I had my own quarters. This dog, a young hound of great promise and very amusing ways, would come for a treat to enjoy the fireside on the hearthrug in my parlour. When I dropped a choice morsel he would invariably follow the zigzag path it had taken, passing his nose backwards and forwards, and come within an inch of the prey, but never attempting to snap it, though it was plain to be seen, and only two inches off. It must be caught by the track, and nothing but the track.

A pet lamb is a poetical subject, but I imagine that even Wordsworth would scarcely have indited a poem on a pet *sheep*. At Steel End Farm, however, where I stayed for a short time, there were two of these useful creatures which had become quite a part of the household. Judging by their condition they must have thought life very well worth living. This old farmhouse, so strikingly situated at the base of Steel Fell, presented a kitchen interior of a wonderfully quaint and primitive character. Just a peep up the steep side of the fell, with the soft light, streaming through the little window in a way that would have delighted Rembrandt, illumining a varied collection of dogs, cats, sheep, and fowls, and the blithe and bonny daughters of the family, radiant with good-humour, passing cheerily to and fro, formed a sight to gladden the heart and amuse the fancy of any chance wanderer over those picturesque solitudes. It seems strange that so few painters seem to have studied these Cumbrian interiors.

Each of the principal farmers keeps a dictionary of sheep marks, a most useful compilation, by which they are enabled to ascertain the owner of any stray animals that appear in their flock. This dictionary, which dates, I believe, from Keswick, works by the system of double marking, viz. by the brand and cutting of the ear. These two marks, with their varieties and combinations, afford a large number of signs. The dictionary, with its illustrations, fills so useful a function that one wonders how matters were adjusted before its introduction. Uncomfortable suspicions as to sheep-stealing must have been more common in the 'pre-dictionary' days than now.

The 'Herdwicks,' as these fell sheep are termed, are a lively race. How comfortably they ensconce themselves among the crags of Wythburn and Borrowdale, cropping the fresh herbage below the jutting crags, and how blithely they skip over the freshly built stone fence, as they contemptuously chuck the rattling stones behind them from off its moss-capped summit !

Many attempts have been made to account for the presence of these Spanish-looking sheep upon the Cumbrian hills, and one of these assigns their origin to their ancestors swimming ashore from the wreck of a ship in the 'Invincible' Armada—a very improbable suggestion. But whatever stock they spring from, there is no question as to the quality of their mutton; well-flavoured, nutritious, and without extra fat, which is doubtless removed by lively exercise upon the fells. Their wool, too, seems very strong and durable. A farmer who wore the produce of his own flock told me that after expenses of spinning, making and trimming were paid (thirty shillings), a suit of good country-spun cloth would last him five or six years. Five shillings a year for cloth. Ponder this, ye beaux of Piccadilly !

CHAPTER VII.

WYTHBURN AND WORDSWORTH—THE WAGGONER— ROCK OF NAMES.

VII.

PASSING over Dunmail Raise, and taking the ancient road on the left, where the incline begins to be steep, you descend, with a long stone fence on your right, to Steel End Farm. This was evidently the most manageable track for making the original road to Westhead and the City, and the primitive settlements on the west side of the valley. After passing Steel End the road dips to a rushing brook, with moss-grown boulders of various sizes scattered along its bed. Looking south-west, you see the recess or 'intake' (pronounce 'intik') that bends inward towards the Langdale Pikes. It is a striking, secluded, and lovely scene. Here is the origin of the Greta, of which this brook is the parent.

Speaking of this stream, in a note upon the sonnet 'To the River Greta, near Keswick,' Wordsworth writes as follows :

'The Cumberland Greta, though it does not among the country people take up *that* name till within three miles of its disappearance in the river Derwent, may

be considered as having its source in the mountain
cove of Wythburn, and flowing through Thirlmere,
the beautiful features of which lake are known only
to those who, travelling between Grasmere and
Keswick, have quitted the main road in the vale of
Wythburn, and crossing over to the opposite side
of the lake, have proceeded with it on the right
hand.'

Wordsworth also mentions the remarkable noises
caused by the concussion of stones in the river-bed
during floods; and Southey quotes, as characteristic
of it, the following lines :

> '. . . Ambiguo lapsu refluitque fluitque
> Occurrensque sibi, venturas aspicit undas.'

Wordsworth's sonnet may be given here :

> 'Greta, what fearful listening ! when huge stones
> Rumble along thy bed, block after block,
> Or, whirling with reiterated shock,
> Combat, while darkness aggravates the groans :
> But if thou (like Cocytus from the moans
> Heard on his rueful margin) thence wert named
> The Mourner, thy true nature was defamed,
> And the habitual murmur that atones
> For thy worst rage, forgotten.   Oft as Spring
> Decks on thy sinuous banks her thousand thrones,
> Seats of glad instinct and love's carolling,
> The concert for the happy then may vie
> With liveliest peals of birthday harmony :
> To a grieved heart thy notes are benisons.'

Into this mountain brook, behind the Nag's Head,
and near the wooden footbridge on the way from

Westhead to Wythburn Church, falls Helvellyn Ghyll. Along its banks the angler may enjoy some of the most remarkable and impressive scenes that Cumbrian mountains can afford. Trout are not large nor plentiful; still they are to be had (by permission of the Manchester Corporation). Wordsworth is quite correct in directing the tourist to the west side of the valley for lovely views, though it must be allowed that the scene from the Cherry Tree towards Dog Ghyll is, in flood-time, singularly attractive.

Over the Greta Brook and the Dog Ghyll the Corporation of Manchester are taking their new road by strong bridges, now probably completed.

The 'Waggoner' is the poem which, 'par excellence,' connects the author of the 'Excursion' with Wythburn.

Never, perhaps, was a poem of humorous incident so completely and exactly descriptive of a journey among the hills as this—a notable instance of the power of poetic genius to cast a halo of glory around the most ordinary occurrences of life. A country carrier proceeding to a distant town along a mountain road is overtaken by a thunderstorm, during which he falls in with a wandering sailor, upon whose wife and child he takes pity and shelters them in his cart. They jog along, companions in misfortune, through the hurly-burly of the elements. Descending into the valley they approach the village inn, from which proceeds the sound of music and the revelry of the

dance.   The temptation is irresistible ; they enter and
join in the revelries.   'It is the village merry night,'
and the sailor by-and-by seizes his opportunity and
produces a model of a man-of-war, which had been
brought there by an ass, and with which he astonishes
Benjamin the carrier and the simple natives of the
vale.   So the fun is kept up and the waggon with
its contents left to take care of itself.

At last they set forth again, the sailor's ass carry-
ing the ship, and the waggoner's mastiff tethered to
the back of the wain.   Morning approaches as they
enter Keswick, and on meeting the master, who has
set forth in search of his man, angry words ensue and
a catastrophe occurs, not only to Benjamin the
waggoner, but to the inhabitants of the vale ; for, as
the poet concludes :

> 'Two losses had we to sustain,
>   We lost both waggoner and wain.'

In this poem — the interest of which is largely
local—one characteristic of Wordsworth is strikingly
illustrated, viz., the faithfulness with which every
topographical feature is seized upon and delineated.
An illustrated edition of it would form an admirable
companion to the tourist in his walk from Rydal to
Keswick.

'Who does not know the famous Swan ?'

From this inn the view towards Langdale as you
sit on the Keswick coach-top is, in certain states of
the atmosphere, simply entrancing.   The variation

of light and shadow and the wonderful fluctuation
and expression of the hill outlines here and about
half way to Dunmail Raise are almost unrivalled.

The Helm Crag, the Astrologer, the Ancient
Woman, 'the Hollow long and bare' by the roadside, the Cairn of King Dunmail, all are accurately
noted in their order, and when the waggoner reaches
the top he hears a female voice imploring help.
Then :

> 'There came a flash, a startling glare,
> And all Seat Sandal is laid bare.'

Seat Sandal is, indeed, *bare* enough at most times,
and these two lines give a curious instance of word-
painting.

Directly after, he hears the woman's husband
calling to him. He had pitched his tent there and
must collect his baggage. Soon they pass 'Wythburn's modest house of prayer.'

If this old church, says the poet,

> ' Had, with its belfry's humble stock,
> A little pair that hang in air,
> Been mistress also of a clock
> * * * * * *
> Twelve strokes that clock would have been telling
> Under the brow of old Helvellyn.'

Then comes the Cherry Tree (now an inn no
longer), and afterwards they pass the spot where was
the 'Rock of Names,' which the reader will find
referred to below.

The dance at the Cherry Tree is a vigorous piece
of description.

> ' Blithe souls and lightsome hearts have we
> Feasting at the Cherry Tree.
> This was the outside proclamation,
> This was the inside salutation.
> What bustling, jostling high and low,
> A universal overflow.
> What tankards foaming from the tap !
> What store of cakes in every lap !
> The Thunder had not been more busy.
> With such a stir you would have said
> This little place may well be dizzy.
> 'Tis—who can dance with greatest vigour?
> 'Tis—what can be most prompt and eager?
> As if it heard the fiddler's call,
> The pewter clatters on the wall ;
> The very bacon shows its feeling,
> Swinging from the smoky ceiling.'

Passing to the poem entitled ' Fidelity,' in which
we have the wonderful endurance of poor Gough's
dog so touchingly described, we get beyond the
confines of the Wythburn parish, if, indeed, the summit of Helvellyn can be considered at all parochial ;
but some traditional explanations of that marvellously
sustained life are still to be had from the ' oldest
inhabitants ' of the valley.   All lovers of animals will
rejoice that a permanent record is now placed in
memory of the devotion of the faithful creature which
originated the beautiful words of the poet concerning
Him

> ' Who gave that strength of feeling great
> Beyond all human estimate.'

Not long ago an anecdote concerning a dog came under the writer's notice, which illustrates fidelity in a striking way. The owner of this creature wished to destroy it, and, taking the animal to the edge of some deep water, made various ineffectual attempts to do so. At last he slipped, and, falling into the stream, nearly lost his life, recovering consciousness upon the bank to find that the animal he had attempted to destroy had saved his own life.

Two poets have sung the praises of poor Gough's companion, and the verses of Scott, perhaps, will long remain better known than ' Fidelity.'

We now pass on to the 'Rock of Names.' After leaving the Cherry Tree, our friend the waggoner and his sailor companion passed the pretty cottage (now Wythburn Post Office) and the spot where recently have stood the navvies' huts. Their course is close by the edge of Thirlmere, and this circumstance calls to the poet's mind the pleasant recollection of the time when he, with near and dear companions carved their initials upon the face of the rock at the roadside. In the note * to the poem of the 'Waggoner,' we find that a passage relating to the 'Rock of Names,' which came after the line, ' Can any mortal clog come to her ?' had been suppressed by Wordsworth. This rock, containing his own initials and those of his friends, was close by the spot where Benjamin is guided

* Moxon's edition, 1845.

6

by the star-glimmer upon the fountain to find the
watering-place.   Thus :

> ' A star declining towards the west
>   Upon the watery surface threw
>   Its image, tremulously imprest,
>   That just marked out the object and withdrew.
>   Right welcome service !   *   *   *
>
>   *   *   *   *   *
>   Rock of Names,
>   Light is the strain but not unjust
>   To thee and thy memorial trust,
>   That once seemed only to express
>   Love that was love in idleness.
>   Tokens, as year hath followed year,
>   How changed, alas, in character !
>   For they were graven on thy smooth breast
>   By hands of those my soul loved best,
>   Meek women, men as true and brave
>   As ever went to a hopeful grave.
>   Their hands and mine, when side by side,
>   With kindred zeal and mutual pride
>   We worked until the Initials took
>   Shapes that defied a scornful look.
>   Long as for us a genial feeling
>   Survives, or one in need of healing,
>   The power, dear Rock, around thee cast.
>   Thy monumental power shall last
>   For me and mine !   Oh thought of pain
>   That would impair it or profane !
>   Take all in kindness then, as said
>   With a staid heart but playful head ;
>   And fail not thou, loved Rock, to keep
>   Thy charge when we are laid asleep.'

Why did the poet suppress these lines ?   Doubtless
on account of the length of the digression they would

have formed in a narrative so short and simple, a digression, too, of a purely personal and subjective kind.

But how full of interest have they now become to us through the lapse of time, and how immensely greater is that interest, as relating to the poet himself than anything that he tells us concerning Benjamin the Waggoner !

During the writer's residence at Wythburn, it fell to his lot to make various inquiries for the welfare of the pieces of this Rock of Names, when removed by the road-makers of the Manchester Corporation. How astonished would Wordsworth have been, if told that this rock would be taken to pieces by navvies, whose work would turn Thirlmere into a reservoir !

May these letters—though it seems much to hope— long be preserved to fulfil the wish of the poet ; conveying, too, to future generations a pleasing memento of the fact that lasting friendship and the kindliest of human sentiments can lodge within a philosopher's breast.

CHAPTER VIII.

CLOUDLAND—LETTER FROM RUSKIN—SUNSET SCENE
FROM WORDSWORTH—CLOUD OUTLINES.

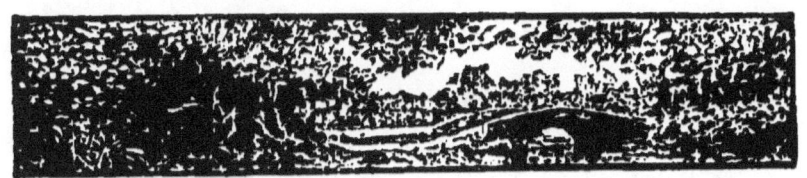

VIII.

EVERY student of modern poetry must be familiar with that marvel of imagination, 'The Cloud,' of Shelley. In the poet's vision the subject of this chapter assumes an individuality which, to some, may appear only imaginative, yet it represents a truth of science.

A cloud is an organism which performs a most important function. Since Luke Howard published early in the present century his tractate containing the classification which has held the field among meteorologists ever since, it is surprising that so little advance should have been made in this study, especially in this matter of classification. The truth seems to be that Howard's types are so obviously natural, and his remarks, generally, so accurately based on real observation, that it is rather extension that is needed than correction of the work of this original observer.

The composition of clouds does not appear to have received the attention which it demands. Not long

ago a London paper published a question relating to
clouds, followed by an answer to it, which began with
the following words : 'Clouds are nothing but fogs
and mists.' This is obviously absurd, and illustrates
forcibly the ignorance that prevails upon the subject.
Not only should the various forms of water, *i.e.*, ice,
sleet, crystals, etc., be taken into the account, but also
the forms of the crystals and particles themselves.
The study of clouds is a wide one. Its importance
has been fully recognised by Prof. Ruskin, one of the
greatest observers of this or any age. In acknow-
ledging a magazine article published by the present
writer a few years ago, Ruskin replied as follows :

'I am extremely glad to see the interest which you
express in clouds. There is no study now open to
you in all the expanse of science where so much can
be done by dexterous attention and patience without
the aid of costly instruments and in the lovely and
healthy laboratory of the air. As you rightly feel,
also, the study is a peculiarly clerical one, whether in
the beauty of its subject or practical use to a country
congregation—sermons in general have too much of
the stars in them, and too little of the weather.'

The interest attaching to this study is fourfold.
Clouds appeal to the artist, the poet, the man of
science, and the divine. Two at least of these fields
are recognised by the author of 'Modern Painters' in
the letter above quoted, as well as in his published
works ; and the pages of Holy Scripture might be

largely quoted—especially the Book of Job and the Psalms—in corroboration of their importance as *spiritual* teachers. It is not a part of our purpose in the present work to dwell on this spiritual aspect of cloudland, as we are now dealing with the phenomena of the physical world; but one striking expression may be cited as showing how clouds affected the imagination of the Hebrew poet of old time.

It is said of the Almighty that 'He maketh the clouds His chariot' (Ps. civ. 3). How striking and how full of consolation is this statement when applied to the antitypes of the clouds, viz., the clouds of sorrow, perplexity, and care among men! In these things Divine providence is as manifest to the eye of faith as is the reign of Divine law in the physical heavens.

The fact that Wordsworth delighted in observing the sky must be evident to all students of his poems. Not only does he paint the cloud appearances by strokes of graphic word-painting in many scenes where other writers would have been content to omit them, but he dwells upon their features in a manner that shows they were to him an essential feature of the landscape. In one passage of the 'Excursion,'* which may justly be termed sublime, he gives a massive and splendid picture of a 'sky revelation,' as it might be termed, which abides in the memory of those that read it.

* Book II., conclusion.

After searching for and finding in the morning mist an old man who had been lost on the mountains, the return journey is begun, and then one of the rescue party describes the sky picture :

> 'A step,
> A simple step that freed me from the skirts
> Of the blind vapour, opened to my view
> Glory beyond all glory ever seen
> By waking sense or by the dreaming soul.
> The appearance instantaneously disclosed
> Was of a mighty city ; boldly say
> A wilderness of building, sinking far
> And self-withdrawn into a boundless depth
> Far sinking into splendour without end.
> Fabric it seemed of diamond and of gold,
> With alabaster domes and silver spires,
> And blazing terrace upon terrace, high
> Uplifted ; here serene pavilions bright
> In avenues disposed ; there towers begirt
> With battlements that on their restless fronts
> Bore stars—illumination of all gems.

> *   *   *   *   *

> Oh, 'twas an unimaginable sight !
> Clouds, mists, streams, watery rocks and emerald turf,
> Clouds of all tincture, rocks and sapphire sky,
> Confused, commingled, mutually inflamed ;
> Molten together, and composing thus
> Each lost in each that marvellous array
> Of temple, palace, citadel and huge
> Fantastic pomp of structure without name
> In fleecy folds voluminous enwrapped.'

> *   *   *   *   *

Such is the manner in which the scenery of cloud-land appeals to the imagination of the poet, and such descriptions are instructive, as illustrating the truth that the sense of beauty is not only a faculty that varies largely in individual natures, but one that is intensified and sublimated by the vitalizing power of circumstances when they kindle a fostering emotion within the soul. It is, as in the incident to which the verses refer, when the feelings are aroused, that Nature presents herself to us in her most transcendental and glorified aspects. It is not merely the material sense that is at work. 'Don't you wish you could, madam?' was the just retort of the painter to the lady who objected that *she* could see no such colours in Nature as he depicted upon his canvas. Tentative, indeed, though the efforts both of painter and poet may often appear, yet they are not on that account ineffectual, for they speak by the power of a kindred and sympathetic instinct to all who possess the sense of natural beauty strong within their souls.

Special phenomena, attractive both to the scientist and the poet, abound undoubtedly in our Lake district. The 'Helm Cloud,' visible on Coniston Old Man, Helvellyn, Skiddaw, and Cross Fell, has been previously spoken of. A kindred appearance, though not perhaps so striking, is the 'Messenger' cloud. This is of a more defined outline and of smaller size than the 'Helm.' Very often it may be observed during and before rainy weather bending at some distance over the summit of a distant peak and deriving an evident correspondence of outline from the configuration of the solid rock beneath it. In texture it generally resembles the kind of stratus that prevails in wet weather in the intervals between showers, but is usually darker in tint and apparently of a looser composition. The interesting problem is to account for the bending over and adapting itself to the form of the mountain, yet remaining at a distance from it. This appearance reminds us that we have not only to allow for the effect of gravitation of the earth *as a planet*, but for the mass attraction of its protuberances, in estimating the forces in operation. Again, that the heat radiation in such cases will be lateral in some degree, as well as vertical ; and last, but not least, that surface currents must at times blow right over the tops of the hills, causing precipitation at a given distance, according to difference of temperature between the current and the lower stratum.

A more striking and curious phenomena is the gradual enveloping of a mountain by a thick envelope of mist which assumes the cirro-cumulus form. This appearance, which I witnessed one evening in autumn from Millom, occurs now and then on Black Comb. From a distance imagination might convert these clouds into a closely-packed flock of gigantic sheep, feeding upon and completely covering the whole upper surface of the hill. The phenomenon is rare.

There can be no doubt that wind often determines the general form of masses of cloud, *e.g.*, the 'anvil' cumulus ; but that it has any considerable influence in originating the main types is doubtful. It is certain that the most satisfactory indications of weather change are to be derived from clouds that have been formed in a comparatively still atmosphere. This fact may be illustrated by observing the piles of cumulus which gather before a thunderstorm, a form of cloud which rarely fails to give a note of warning when the storm is still distant.

Cloud outlines next claim our attention.

By the outline of a cloud we may readily distinguish its class and peculiar characteristics. Although the term 'cumulus' (a mass) does not indicate so well as the names of Howard's other two types the form which it presents to the eye, the varieties of the cloud are, by outline alone, more distinctly defined than those of any other. It would be possible to form a classification of the various species of the cloud almost entirely by their outlines.

We select two forms, both valuable as weather prognostics, to illustrate the use of observing outlines. The first is the Electric Cumulus,* and the second the Anvil Cloud of Sir J. Herschell. The outline of the electric cumulus is very sharp and hard, not broken by large indentations and loose feathery processes like that of the commoner kinds of cumulus, formed rapidly by exhalations from the earth, and drifting near its surface; but we have almost a con-

* Described by the writer in the *Quarterly Journal of the Brit. Meteor. Society,* Jan., 1872.

tinuous line, often terminating in stratus or nimbus
below, yet rising to a vertex, conical or rounded, with
small curves and minute projections, showing the
rounded protuberances on the surface of the cloud.

There is no cloud that possesses a more distinct
outline than this, and none which exhibits more
brilliant effects of light.   As a weather-prognosticator
it is best observed at a distance, and near the horizon,
when the form of the summit may be more exactly
discerned.

We now consider the Anvil Cloud.

This species, alluded to by Sir John Herschell in his
'Familiar Lectures on Science,' cannot be regarded as
so strictly a form of cumulus as that which we have
just noticed, inasmuch as it exhibits at times a great
tendency to the form of stratus, and occasionally to
that of cirrus ; or, perhaps we should rather say, to the
form of cumulo-cirrus.*   As an indicator of wind, this
cloud may probably be regarded as unrivalled.   It
frequently appears two or three days before heavy
gales, especially when they are of long duration, as
about the Equinoxes.   Without being hypercritical,
we may distinguish three varieties of the cloud, the
outlines of which are characteristic.   The first variety
possesses greater affinity for ordinary cumulus than the
other two, and it often shows great resemblance in

---

* This cloud, also an excellent indicator of wind, does not
appear to have received the attention it deserves from meteorologists.   The reader must not confound it with cirro-cumulus.

many points to the electric cumulus. It occurs for the most part in large masses or banks, the summits of which as it drifts along with the wind, stand out in sharp relief against the upper sky, and exhibit the most striking and fantastic resemblances to terrestrial objects, beetling crags, towers, and heads of animals—the last being of frequent occurrence. When of this variety, the anvil cloud appears to be highly condensed, and is of a dark bluish or slatey tint. It is generally, I believe, the precursor of heavy rain as well as wind.

The second variety of the cloud, which approaches to stratus, exhibits a more irregularly formed 'anvil,' the ' waist' being usually much more conspicuous on one side than on the other. This is also a dense cloud, without much marking on its surface, the outline being not nearly so irregular as that of the variety just described. It is of a lighter tint, gray or muddy bluish, and does not, I think, occur in an isolated form, but rises from a bank of lower stratus or cumulostratus. It is also a wet-weather cloud.

The third variety is a kind of aggregated cirrus, generally of a dark tint, and seen at high altitudes in windy weather. This lacks the consistency and volume of ordinary cumulus, and spreads itself out almost in a sheet, with rounded edges, and without surface marking.

The year 1872 was remarkable both for its excessive rainfall and the number and destructive violence of its thunderstorms. It was equally remarkable for the variety and striking character of its cloud forms. The electric cumulus was scarcely absent for a day during the whole period over which the thunderstorms extended. On one occasion, when leaving Liverpool for Blackburn, I observed three or four conical piles of the cloud upon the horizon in the direction of the latter town; the weather was beautiful at Liverpool, but a storm, as I learnt on arriving at my destination, had raged there at the time I observed the cloud so many miles away.

There can be little doubt that this phenomenon may often be seen at a distance of 50 to 100 miles from the point where the storm breaks.

Another remarkable form that appeared during the summer of 1872 was the 'Festooned' or Pocky Cloud, as some have termed it. Professor Poey some years ago alluded to it as a 'new' variety. Since then, however, it has been shown to be of ancient date, and a somewhat elaborate and interesting account of earlier observations was contributed by Mr. Scott to the *Quarterly Journal of the Meteorological Society*, April, 1872. I have myself observed the cloud on several occasions, though only once or twice in perfect form. The droplets or festoons which form the lower outline of the cloud have a semi-elliptical or egg-shaped form, were very dark, and extended over a considerable portion of the heavens. In the most perfect example noted by me (about twenty years ago), the pendulous processes or droplets had an almost perfectly circular outline, even, and well defined. The festoons were about four or five degrees in apparent diameter, their altitude being perhaps a mile. The whole mass from which the droplets depended was not large, and moved with the wind, the curves meanwhile retaining their form intact. What made the case most singular was, that the regularity of the outline could be maintained, even a few moments, under the variable atmospheric conditions of the time. Though the outlines were so regular, the surface of the cloud had a very nimbus-like appearance, and was of a lurid yellow tint. The sky was not overcast at the time.

The more usual concomitants of this form are, how-ever, a dark turbid sky and a ' pallium' of cirro-cumulus subsiding into nimbus or nimbo-stratus. Under these conditions I observed it twice during the stormy summer of 1871, one of the cases being immediately after a thunderstorm. The fact of its being emphatically a foul-weather cloud adds interest to the investigation, for heavy rain and wind usually follow its appearance. My own observations indicate, however, that rain is more certain to follow than wind. In Lancashire it is sometimes termed ' rain-ball.'

The origin of these symmetrical cloud-forms is very difficult to determine. Mr. Scott, in his paper above referred to, attaches considerable importance to the experiments of Sir J. Herschell and Mr. Jevons, by whom it has been shown that a similar appearance may be produced by gradually mixing two fluids of slightly different specific gravities.

The nature, however, of the forces which determine the peculiar symmetry of such forms seems almost equally obscure in the case of the experiments as in that of the atmospheric phenomenon they are used to illustrate.

CHAPTER IX.

INVERTED PYRAMID CUMULUS—DROPPING CUMULUS—
FESTOON CLOUD—HIGH RAIN-CUMULUS—LAW OF
ALTITUDES—HAIL AND SNOW CLOUDS.

IX.

WE now call attention to a cloud which may be denominated 'pyramid cumulus.' Strictly speaking, it should be *inverted* pyramid cumulus, as the point or apex is generally turned downwards toward earth, or inclined at an angle with the horizon. The mass of the cloud, which is often very irregularly shaped at the larger end, partakes for the most part largely of the character of stratus or nimbus, and the surface is often marked by sinuous lines, which radiate from the inverted apex upwards.

The cases in which I have observed this form of cloud have generally been during a thunderstorm, about its climax, or after the rain has begun to fall. One of the most striking occurred during a storm which discharged itself about thirty miles from the point of observation. Like the ordinary electric cumulus,* the pyramid cumulus sometimes rises to a great elevation, and is visible at a vast distance, when the lightning may be seen darting and playing about

* See *Journal of Meteor. Soc.*, January, 1872.

its surface, thus indicating the violence of the storm over which it hovers, while the weather in the neighbourhood of the observer may be perfectly fine.*

The cloud derives interest from its evident connection with that conical or funnel-shaped form of cumulus which attends the formation of a waterspout, and thus gives an indirect confirmation to the theory that this latter phenomenon is a result of electrical action. It seems quite evident that the violent action, both on the water and on the atmosphere, which is exerted by a waterspout, and the tremendously rapid movement of the particles, can only result from the presence of a force acting with enormous power from molecule to molecule.

To afford a *raison d'être* for this phenomenon, and for that of the sand-pillar, from the ordinary mechanical laws regulating large masses of air, seems an obvious impossibility. But it may be objected that, if the pyramid cumulus and other cognate cloud forms are due to electric action of the air or vapour particles, how does it happen that the surface of these clouds and their general contour do not change more rapidly? To this it may be replied, that if an observer were so placed as to obtain a distinct and near view of the component particles of the cloud, he might (and probably would) observe a very rapid motion among them. For at a distance of several miles appearances

* A case of this kind occurred about the year 1869, and was described by me in the *Intellectual Observer.*

are very deceptive as to material composition,* movement of particles, etc. ; and it is also plain that identity
of visible form at two different moments is no proof
whatever of an identity of component particles. Take,
for example, the rainbow, which exhibits such exquisite
symmetry and such apparent stability of form as
altogether to preclude the idea of change or motion,
while it is well known that the bow and its colouring
are due to refraction of light through a constant
succession of falling drops, so that not only do two
persons see different rainbows, but no one can see
the same rainbow two moments together.

In the symmetrical marking which the pyramid
cumulus occasionally assumes, we have a remarkable
resemblance to the form taken by the whirling sand-
pillar of the desert. A whirlwind is evidently the
originating force, but whether the direction of the
currents is originally upwards or downwards I must
leave to other observers to determine. Some persons
seek an explanation of these forms in the action of
two vapour currents of different densities meeting
each other; but in the cases we have just considered,
where a rapid motion is observed, the atmosphere all
around being still, we may perhaps find a solution in
the generation of electricity by heat or evaporation.

---

* A singular phenomenon may often be noticed in connection
with rain, which has not been fully explained, viz., the *darting*
to and fro of small particles among the larger drops, like minute
snowflakes flitting about in defiance of gravitation.

The 'festoon' cloud, which is commonly seen before squally weather and with a falling temperature, may, however, be due to ascending currents of vapour meeting colder currents of air descending towards the earth.

We now examine the 'dropping' cumulus. I am not aware that previous writers have considered this a distinct species; but it deserves to be so recognised for two reasons, viz., its value as a weather prophet (indicating wind and rain), and the curious inquiries which it suggests concerning the coherence of cloud masses, and the relation which the forces that determine this coherence bear to that of gravitation. A very ancient writer * has pointed out the scientific problems involved in this adjustment of mechanical laws, as yet far from solution.

There is a close affinity between this form and the 'festoon' cloud. The latter ought perhaps to be regarded as a variety of the 'dropping' cumulus. The most curious characteristic of the cloud we are now considering is its manner of hanging down endwise towards the earth. It appears at times to have a hollow space within; for a kind of outward shell may be seen to form in the first instance, gradually developing from a vapoury strip or band, and rapidly assuming a semi-cylindrical shape (almost that of a bolster), and acquiring at last a full rotundity of outline. I have observed several masses formed in

* Book of Job, chap. xxxvii., v. 16.

this way, parallel to each other, and all in different stages of development.

Among the accidental varieties of 'dropping' cumulus, two curious forms may be noted, viz., that of a double cone and of a dumb-bell. The last-mentioned may be closely allied to the 'anvil' cloud, but is looser in texture and generally more rapid in motion and change of form.

It has been remarked by some observers that the characteristics of the rarer clouds are very *local*, but it must be borne in mind that the same result will be observed where the conditions are the same.

There seems to be a difference in the average altitude of clouds on the west and east coasts of England, those of the latter having the greater eleva-tion. The estuaries of the Mersey and of the Dee present a very interesting field of observation; the varieties of cloud being numerous, the changes of form rapid, and the gradations of colouring and of light and shade rich and deep. To account for these phenomena we have: 1. The irregularity of the coast-line, with two considerable rivers lying close together. 2. The hills of North Wales. 3. The intermingling of currents, and the evaporation from the Gulf Stream. The part of east Kent, viz., that between Sandwich and Dover, presents finer effects in the rich glow of the upper sky, especially before sunrise and after sun-set; a clear yet soft and rich golden light, into the depths of which the eye seems to penetrate, at times intensely beautiful. This glow was seen on several occasions in November, 1877. The purity and depth of the ruby-tinted cirro-stratus at sunset is also very noticeable. The fine effects of cloud about Liverpool were, I believe, well known to the great painter Turner, who spent many a day making studies in the district. The excess of vapour arising from flats and sand-banks gives a hazy and delicate effect to the light, very suggestive in a picture.

With regard to these differences of atmospheric effect caused by change of locality, it appears that such change is found rather in the grouping, elevation and effects of light and colour, than in the forms themselves, though there are certain forms, no doubt, quite local, especially in mountainous districts. These generally owe their origin to geographical configuration, and their study lies as much within the province of the physical geographer as that of the meteorologist. The curious disc or cap which is seen near the peak of some mountains, and which maintains its form in a breeze of wind, *must* have its particles in rapid motion ; being caused by the continuous impact of vapour currents upon a colder stratum, which determines condensation and visibility. This is a good example of the principle stated above, that identity of visible form at two different moments is no proof of identity in the particles. The flame of a candle, which cannot, chemically, remain the same two moments together, affords also an illustration of this. A cloud,

like the human body, may often be likened to an
eddy. Physiology teaches us that the body is sustained
by a constant motion of particles absorbed from ex-
ternal sources and passed off again after undergoing a
change of form ; yet no one doubts that he possesses
the same body which he had, say, ten years ago.
The saying that 'sameness' must not be confounded
with 'thisness' and 'thatness' (or identity) in its strict
sense, is applicable in both cases. Every cloud, as
has been remarked by Espy, is either a forming or a
dissolving one; but I think we may extend this, and
say that some clouds are both 'forming' and 'dissolving' at the same time ; *e.g.*, cirro-cumulus, forming
from cirrus and melting into nimbus.

But we now pass on to consider a form of cumulus
which is associated with very wet weather, and which
I do not think has yet had a distinguishing title
accorded to it. This I propose to call the 'High rain-
cumulus.' It is not a common species, and is mostly
seen in autumn and spring. It deserves the name
that I have given it, on account of the tremendously
heavy showers that attend its appearance, and the
great elevation which it often attains. Unlike most
forms of cumulus, which it is best to observe when
somewhat near the horizon, so that the vertex may be
seen in outline, this cloud reveals its characteristics
best when almost overhead. Let the reader picture
to himself a mild, muggy day in spring or autumn ;
everything soaking with recent showers, with heavy,

lumpy-looking masses hanging about the horizon, and a drift of flattish, irregular cirro-cumulus occupying the upper stratum.*   Some of the masses of cumulus will be observed to throw off limbs or projections which swell out, and, ascending almost to the upper drift, seem to creep over the zenith much in the manner of a thunder-cloud when the electricity is gathering just over the place of observation.   The cloud then forms into a kind of sheet (as seen from below) with rounded outline, and the edge broken with many small, curling indentations, somewhat like the leaves of some plants.   The lower portion has a flat appearance, as if repelled rather than attracted by the earth.   The elevation is considerable, and the tint of the cloud a dirty gray or slate-colour.

This kind of cloud frequently forms in enormous masses, as may be seen from its great altitude, and the manner in which the sheet extends towards the horizon ; but, though much flatter in form than most varieties of cumulus, its surface is often broken or nodulous, like that of hail cumulus or electric cumulus when these are ready to discharge their contents.   The peculiar form of this species is probably due in part to the saturated condition of the lower atmosphere at the time of its occurrence, and I have given to it the special designation of 'rain' cumulus to indicate the

---

* See remarks below on the relative height of different species of cloud.

excessively wet weather that it is generally associated with. ·

One of the most remarkable facts in connection with atmospheric phenomena is this—that certain characteristic forms of cloud find their habitat within a certain zone, or at certain distances from the earth's surface. Omitting stratus, we find them usually in the following order, ascending from the earth: (i.) Cumulus; (ii.) Cirro-cumulus; (iii.) Cirrus. The second of these appears to be an intermediate stage between cirrus, the ice-cloud in its normal state, and cumulus; or between cirrus and nimbus; and it has a very great range of altitude. Thus it might appear to be an exception to the law—that *form* depends partly on elevation; but it will, I think, be admitted that, as a general rule, it occupies a region lying between that of the other two species. But besides altitude there are doubtless relations existing between the banks of cloud themselves which affect the question of form. This especially would be the case where there was strong interchange of electrical action.

But whatever may be the cause of the law we speak of, this fact deserves attention, that any decided deviation from the law is significant of a disturbed condition of the atmosphere, and often is indicative of approaching storms. Let us take two cases to illustrate this; in very thundery weather the two great types of cloud show a tendency to interchange their places in regard to altitude; that is to say, cumulus rises to an abnormal height, and cirrus descends to an unusually low position. This may generally be verified by watching the course of a thunderstorm; when the peaks of the first-mentioned cloud may often be observed at a great distance thrusting their pale yellow pinnacles into the azure of the heavens, long before the first muttering of the storm is heard, and while the mass of cloud is far beyond the horizon. On the other hand, when the hurly-burly is over and the rain has ceased, masses of nimbo-cirrus may at times be seen throwing up their silvery crests, and curling over the earth like gigantic breakers. This last-mentioned appearance, which has a splendid effect, is, I believe, never seen except in thundery weather, or rather during electrical disturbance, and it is not easy to account for the existence of such forms by the action of wind. The last remark applies also to what we may call 'star' cirrus; that is, cirrus streaks radiating from a common centre in all directions (a form of cloud also connected with thunderstorms), and to that form which resembles the feathering of an arrow, parallel rays running from both sides of a common axis.*

'We shall have stormy weather, sir; those animal clouds have been seen again to-day.' Such was the remark made to me by a countrywoman in Kent, and

* Observations made continually during many years since this law of interchange of altitudes was first noticed by me in the *Popular Science Review*, have fully confirmed the truth of the foregoing remarks concerning its relation to atmospheric disturbance.

this observation was true enough to nature ; it agreed also with my own notes at the time on the appearance of 'anvil cloud,' or fracto-cumulus. 'Ram's-head' cloud might not inappropriately be the term used to describe this drifting bank of hail or rain, which often marks the sky with such striking and fantastic outlines. Observe these dark rolling masses at sunset on an autumn afternoon, and see what kind of weather the night brings with it—driving sleet and sudden gusts of wind, with 'bursts' of hail rising often to a furious and full-blown nor'wester, which make one thankful for a good roof overhead.

The general form and type of the 'hail cloud' is pretty well known to observers of atmospheric pheno-mena. In most cases it greatly resembles the snow-cumulus, though generally more craggy in outline, harder in its edges, and more attended by stratus* at its base. There are, however, several types of snow-cloud. When drifting against a clear sky, the latter presents a more fleecy and softer edging, though in its general form it must be grouped, like that which originates hail-showers, with the class of 'animal' cloud, *i.e.*, condensed† fracto-cumulus. Both of these are again closely akin to the electric cumulus or cone cloud (see *Science Gossip* for July, 1879). Here we

---

* This indicates a closer affinity with the rain-cloud, or nimbus.

† This is the term adopted by Professor Poëy, and indicates a mass broken by wind.

ought to note the frequent connection existing between the hail-shower and electrical discharges, and the part that electricity is known to play in the condensation and cohesion of the watery particles.

Let us notice now that a law seems to hold good in regard to the origin of the different forms of cloud, through which it is possible to forecast weather by observing them. This is 'a law of correspondence' between the particles composing a cloud and the general form of the mass. It varies its manifestations with the temperature and other physical conditions of the medium in which the vapoury particles are floating; yet the principle involved in the connection between the form of the body and the molecules which compose it is constant; it depends upon the manner of their aggregation.

It is a physical or chemical question to determine the special forms that will be originated by given component particles under given physical conditions. To determine such resultant forms in the case of previously unknown substances, is a problem difficult in the highest degree, and I suppose practically insoluble in the generality of instances, except where an approximating form may be guessed at, by witnessing the evolutions that result from analogous substances.

To forecast, for example, the general form which would be assumed by an aggregation of the crystals of some hitherto uncompounded chemical, would be an impossibility, except by examining the effect of known combinations almost similar in composition.

Still more difficult would it be to suggest the form likely to be taken by a tree, from an examination of the seed, though even here analogy might suggest something. But it could suggest nothing as to the reason of their taking the particular form under observation. The seeds of two different plants may be exceedingly alike in general structure and composition, yet the form of their leaves and stem will present the widest possible diversity.

Yet in considering the process of growth, we must not overlook the variety of elements which may be absorbed from the earth and atmosphere. It is not a question of the simple evolution of a given material into an organism from a given embryo, but of the drawing into a focus or vortex a great variety of elements, operated on by an almost equal variety of forces. The laws which regulate the operation of those forces are the laws which originate the various forms that meet our eyes, and produce a resulting structure characterized by permanence and beauty.

An Owen may rebuild, from the fragments presented to him, the frame of a being long extinct, whose remains lie embedded in the bowels of the earth, and we accept his construction because we believe it to be based on the order of nature shown by the exact observation of analogous forms. But even Owen's efforts to reconstruct would be simply

8

abortive, and the result a falsity, were it not for the permanence and continuity of law in Nature. Without the operation of fixed law within the component particles, no species, either in the animal or vegetable world, could possess continuity of form.

It is sufficient for our present purpose to direct attention to the relation existing between 'mass' and 'particle.' But it is also necessary to point out that there must always be a great defect in the value of illustrations from the mixing of liquids of different density, such as those adduced by the late Professor Jevons. Interesting as these experiments are, the movements and elasticity of the atmosphere vary too greatly from those of liquids to allow experiments in mixing to be of much practical value in regard to ascertaining the causes of the forms of cloud.

Suffice it to remark that, inasmuch as the form of the mass largely depends on the nature of the particles— whether ice, snow, sleet, hail, or rain—we have probably in the particular forms which the mass assumes an adequate reason for the belief that weather may be forecasted from them.

CHAPTER X.

X.

OF the three main types of cloud, Cirrus, Cumulus, and Stratus, there is none which presents greater diversities of form and more interesting problems in physical research than the cirrus.

Ornamenting as it does the highest reaches of the upper sky with its pure and graceful feathery and flower-like figures, and forming by its transitional modification so great a number of unlooked-for and attractive combinations, it has always been a favourite with the student of weather, and has afforded to the tourist and pedestrian a source of infinite amusement and speculation.

The remarks now given on this cloud are based on observations extending over many years. The subject is admitted to be a difficult one, yet it is surprising how much misconception has become current respecting this form of cloud. For example, in a popular educational work on 'Physiography,' in use in national schools, the writer seems to be under the impression that cirrus has a tendency to lie in certain defined positions, as N.N.E. or S.S.W., etc., and it is suggested that this is due to some regular currents of the upper atmosphere. Now the fact is well known to any moderately informed observer of clouds that cirrus has *no fixed direction* at all, nor any tendency to take one, *but lies in any direction whatever*, and that also in the most eccentric way, so that the ingenious author of the above-named explanation is very much in the same position as certain philosophers when endeavouring, at the waggish instance of Charles II., to account for a phenomenon that was non-existent.

The truth is that Nature is infinitely wider, far more varied in her forms, and far more subtle in her operations than most of us are aware of. One of the cardinal vices of a science which only deserves the name of ' pseudo-science,' but which does duty with a vast number of untrained minds, is the building of systems and the over-free use of technical or special nomenclature. I use the word technical, yet it must be pointed out that ' technical ' does not apply here exactly as in more defined sciences. Take the word oxygen. Every chemist at once understands by this word a gas possessing certain properties that recur to his memory whenever he uses the word. It is not so with such terms as occur in treating of the forms of cloud, *e.g.*, cumulo-cirro-stratus. Such compound terms may represent a variety of forms according to the *extent* to which each type of cloud is represented in the given expression ; thus a ' cumulo-cirro-stratus ' might be more or less of cumulus, cirrus, or of stratus in any particular instance, so that the forms represented by this *one expression* might vary considerably and indefinitely.

It is obvious, therefore, that if any headway is to be made in the study of clouds it must be by a larger and more exact acquaintance with actual forms rather than by ingenious attempts at fresh nomenclature. Every modification, even the most minute and delicate, represents some force or other at work in the air around; it may be heat, cold, wind, gravitation, electricity, or perhaps earth-magnetism; but whatever the force may be, it has a distinct action on the particles of the cloud, and the cloud in its turn is a clear index to the existence and operation of these forces.

It is just this fact which renders the accumulated stores of weather lore possessed by gamekeepers, sailors, farmers, etc., so valuable. Though often deficient in power of description, men whose occupation partly compels them to a study of natural phenomena often acquire a very considerable acquaintance with the forms and phenomena presented to them. Accurate observation and a retentive memory will give a store of forms and data which may constitute the basis of formulated science. But the want of a trained reasoning faculty makes such weather lore empirical, and the want of a power of exact expression limits its value to the individual.

At the same time this simple connotation of facts

and local appearances will be of far more use than the mere building up theories, or the invention of a technical jargon based on the observations of other people. It matters little how familiar the expression, or whether the language be Latin, French, or English, so long as it is accurately used, and does duty for an actual phenomenon. Consequently, if the phrase 'Ram's-head cloud' or 'Bead cloud' pictures a given type better than 'Fracto-cumulus' or 'Stratiforial-cumulus,' I should have no hesitation in using it. With regard to such terms as 'Stratiforius' and 'Cumuliforius,' suggested by a certain author in *Science Gossip*, January, 1888, it is hard to see how science, which is the understanding of facts, can be advanced by extending the use of Latin or Greek terminology. My own aim is to induce others to observe the wonders of the sky for themselves.

The writer referred to, in criticising my articles on the 'Types of Storm Cloud,' seems to wish to omit cirrus altogether as a type of cloud forming a class. But cirrus as truly forms a class of cloud as cumulus itself. It can never be classified as a variety of cumulus or stratus. It differs from stratus in its composition, and undoubtedly consists of ice. This has been shown repeatedly by its optical effects, and confirmed by the researches of balloonists.

If we are to have two main classes, and not the three suggested by Luke Howard, they will un-doubtedly be represented by 'cumulus' and 'cirrus,' or 'ball cloud' and 'hair cloud,' corresponding to 'vapour' and 'ice.'

'Stratus,' or 'flat' and 'straight' forms, together with the various compound forms 'cirro-stratus' and 'cumulo-cirro-stratus' will then find their proper place as transitional modifications. I may notice that these 'transitional modifications' and composite varieties afford most interesting subjects for speculation, and indicate in a striking manner the variety of forces at work upon the watery vapour during weather change. To these various forces, coupled with the molecular properties both of ice and water, are due the innumerable varieties of cloud scenery; but the attempt to group all the forms of cloud under two such terms as 'cumuliforius' and 'stratiforius' as suggested above would be, to my mind, about as logical as to invent two fine terms, and then endeavour to arrange the whole animal kingdom under them.

This is playing Procrustes with a vengeance in order to make science 'easy.' But 'vaporology,' as Professor Ruskin terms it, can never be made easy in this way. It demands, not only a good general knowledge of physics, but considerable reasoning power and a capacious memory.

Cirrus at its greatest elevation sometimes presents curves of great beauty. One of these resembles the letter S, thick in the middle and tapering to the ends. The cloudlets lie somewhat apart.

I call this 'double curve' cirrus. It may be termed

a modification of the cloud called in popular parlance 'Mackerel Scales.' No doubt it is a transitional modification, indicating a disturbed state of atmosphere. One side of the cloud is firmly defined, the other softly brushed away, so as to blend imperceptibly with the blue of the sky.

This cloud I have classed with cirrus on account of its great *altitude* and its curvilinear form. Others might be disposed to rank it with cirro-cumulus, inasmuch as it is composed of separate cloudlets aggregated together. The matter of altitude has unfortunately been taken too little count of by meteorologists, in regard to cloud classification, and this is the more remarkable as altitude, by causing variation of temperature, generally determines the crystalline or non-crystalline form of atmospheric vapour. This fact appears to me of such importance that it should form the basis of *classification ;* heat and cold being the primary factors of molecular condition, and these forces being regulated by distance from the earth.

Thus we might have first, second, and third 'zone' clouds, corresponding to cumulus, composite forms, and cirrus.

With regard to the origin of this double curve cirrus, a spirally moving current might be suggested. It may be classified with 'storm clouds,' like the patches of parallel stratus known by the name of 'hen scarts,' which *when seen in the upper zone* should be regarded as straight cirrus; so also may the 'mackerel scales' just referred to, being generally at a great altitude. 'Mackerel scales' may be regarded as 'single' curve cirrus; 'double' curve cirrus being a variety of the same cloud arising from a more complicated current or movement.

The most remarkable case of 'double curve' cirrus observed by me was followed by stormy, wet weather.

It may be taken as an axiom of weather forecasting that small patches of well-defined and oddly-shaped clouds of the cirrus or cirro-cumulus type generally indicate stormy and changeable weather.

With regard to spiral currents of air in the upper drift, I may say that the forms which they seem responsible for, *e.g.*, 'twist' or 'screw'* cloud, are nearly always followed by rain or wind and rain. The ordinary type of cirrus, so common in fine summer weather, is of a much flatter form and looser structure than those now referred to.

These curiously formed patches appear to attain the greatest height of any forms *visible from the earth.*† In passing I may note that the highest cloud ever observed by me was a very beautiful layer of cirro-

---

* The term 'curl' cloud has been adopted by so many writers generically for cirrus, that I avoid its use here. 'Ringlet' would be more exact than 'screw' for this variety.

† All ordinary forms of cloud appear blue when elevated to a sufficient distance from the observer. The highest clouds seen from a balloon are probably quite invisible from the earth, being tinted blue by distance.

cumulus sprinkled over the upper heavens, resembling pale blue pellets of snow, almost blended in tint with the blue heaven above. Just as the most distant stars are shrouded in the abyss of space, so the highest forms of cloud disappear in the azure distance of the sky. We must not forget that there are visible clouds and invisible.

Visibility frequently depends upon position with regard to the sun or moon, as the case may be. On a moonlight night, especially in stormy weather, clouds may be seen to become visible just as they approach the angular position of the ordinary halo (60°). Then they pass from sight again when that position is passed, and the refraction is unnoticed. Sometimes a circular ring of matted cirrus appears about the sun or moon for a considerable time, caused solely by the fact of its position with respect to the source of light corresponding to the angular distance above mentioned. Similar phenomena occur, too, in connection with coronæ, which depend upon the lesser refractive power of water.

In considering these and kindred phenomena we should not forget the prodigious amount of vapour floating above us, and the calculation of an eminent astronomer, that if all this vapour held in solution by the atmosphere were precipitated, twenty feet or more of snow would very soon cover the whole surface of the earth.

As local notes are usually valued by students of

science, I will give here a few observations relating to
the crystalline and semi-crystalline clouds of the upper
drift (cirrus, cirro-stratus, and cirro-cumulus) taken in
the vicinity of Helvellyn during the remarkably wet
summer of 1890.

From May to August the weather was almost con
tinual wet, a single fine day occurring, however, at
times. For the most part, the sky resolved itself into
two distinct *pallia*, represented by rolling cumulus and
cumulo-nimbus in the lower drift, which was but little
removed above the mountain top, and, in the upper
drift, the above-mentioned crystalline forms, which
almost invariably appeared when the lower drift broke
for a brief interval of fair weather.

The appearance of these cloudlets was *almost invariably* the signal for another wet day immediately
following.

Their forms were very varied, but two generic types
were for the most part predominant, viz., the 'hen
scart' or short parallel cirro-stratus, usually thought to
denote wind; and the 'honeycomb' form of cirro-
cumulus, which often covers a considerable portion of
the sky.

Patches of cirrus overlaid one upon another, apparently adhering and moving together in one system,
were often seen. These patches maintain their shape
in a wonderful manner in the face of the wind, and
their form can scarcely be accounted for by wind
alone. The 'honeycomb' type of cirrus is transitional,

and seems to represent the first formation of a bank of cirro-cumulus.

If the sudden re-arrangement of particles, which we call crystallization, is determined by electricity, and if this again be dependent on earth magnetism, we have a chain of connection between 'cosmic' force and the daily change of weather.   We cannot but believe that 'law' operates in every movement of the atmosphere as much as among the stars ; yet, how unaccountable many cloud movements are !   How many theories have been advanced with regard to the stratified and aggregated forms called Noah's Ark !

These long bands of cirro-stratus and straight-cirrus (forming really an extended oblong pallium) almost invariably were followed by a wind that blew at right angles, or nearly so, to the line of the cloud.

This special form of pallium, which is doubtless transitional, corresponds, it may be, with a zone of magnetic influence, as above suggested.   It certainly has a tendency to north and south direction, at least in Wythburn Valley; but to say that cirrus generally has any particular direction is erroneous.

Space forbids that I should here attempt a new theory of classification.   Let me rather exhort all observers of clouds to accurately note the outline, volume, colouring, manner of aggregation, and especially the *elevation* of each type which they undertake to examine.

Accurate observations are the substance ; classification is, after all, but a shadow, a process of human imagination. The very unity and immensity of physical law forbids the completion of theories with respect even to a section of her domain, and reverence demands that we should continue with much patience our researches in so wide a field, never forgetting the exhortation of the poet of Rydal Mount :

' Let Nature be your teacher.'

For Nature is herself neither more nor less than

' The art of God.'

CHAPTER XI.

CAIRN OF DUNMAIL—NATURE, NORMAL AND AB-
NORMAL—BARROWS—THE FARMER'S TOILS—SOME
LOCAL NAMES—CITY OR SITTING?

XI.

PASSING over the desolate height of Dunmail
Raise one summer afternoon (1890) we observed, as the coach skirted the well-known cairn of
the Cumbrian warrior—

      ' Last King of rocky Cumberland,'

a labourer busy in the centre of the heap, erecting a
monument as an ornament, with the stones lying
around him. This ornament was a sort of pyramid,
surmounted by a knob, that suggested a huge tobacco
jar. Ornamenting a cairn! What would the poets
have said to this?

What shapes must have visited that unhappy mortal
in the silent watches of the ensuing night? Turning
to him, as the coach passed by, our driver, with
expressive look and warning tone, called out from
his box: 'Take care the old gentleman don't come
up!' There was a sarcasm on his grave face, and a
droll turn in that driver's neck quite noteworthy for
a Northern Jehu.

That knobby pyramid's day was of short duration, and a poet's remonstrance was said to have been the efficacious power of removal—removal that restored to the ancient pile its poetry once more. All honour be accorded to the poet; for not many are the kingly monuments that Cumbria can boast !

This is the spot that bears the grim and gruesome record that Edmund, the Saxon King, defeated (A.D. 945) the last monarch of the Celts—Dunmail or Dumhnail—slew him, and cruelly put out the eyes of his two sons.

> ' A cruel place to dout* a mortal's eyes,
>   So fair the scene, yet here the deed was done !
>   Cast, with a sigh, the tributary stone
>   For those two sons whose sire hereunder lies.
>   That day when Edmund, with victorious cries,
>   Stormed up the pass and broke gray Cumbria's throne,
>   He little thought those blinded boys had won
>   The surer realm where pity never dies.
>   And those brave lads, whose only fault was this—
>   They helped their father for the British right,
>   Hot on their eyes the brand might sear and hiss
>   And bring with pain of hell unending night,
>   But better blindly grope the mountain ways
>   Than see the Saxon over Dunmail Raise.'
>
>   H. D. RAWNSLEY.

The boundary that divides Westmorland and Cumberland, passes along the brook beside this cairn and through the cairn itself, hence the desire in some quarters to make the pile still more conspicuous. But

* Dout = do out, *cf.* doff.

the cairn and its memory will probably survive when, should the world last so long, the Manchester Water Works have become a mysterious antiquity of the hoary past.

The efforts of man to mark the features on Nature's face and to intensify her lessons, sometimes of long duration, though for the most part soon swept away or metamorphosed by the forces that surround them, are themselves a part of her own operation. Why should an ant-hill or the house of a beaver be regarded as the handiwork of Nature, and not so the cairn of a warrior or the mausoleum of a statesman? The 'evolutionist' will echo Why, indeed? but the moralist will point out how vastly different is the effect upon the lines of beauty and grace, and will tell you that ugliness and sin go hand in hand, and that there is a screw loose in *man's* machinery. He will take you to the slums of Whitechapel, or to the 'pandemoniac' atmosphere of Chemicopolis, and ask you, If *that* is Nature, what must be the need of revelation when Nature abnormal differs from Nature normal by such a gulf? Are not man and Nature, though he be her son, too often conflicting elements? Are not his proudest works too often a painful illustration of the truth that while beauty is skin deep, ugliness may be bone deep?

But that beautifying and softening power that moderates the hideousness of man's monstrosities, and humiliates the excrescences that he dignifies with the title of Architecture, is mighty, and, like Truth, will prevail. It is not merely an enduring force in the elements that surround us, but a permanent quality in the very structure of their atoms. Not more surely does oxygen effect its protean migrations from sea to cloud, from cloud to tree, from tree to earth or air, and from earth or air to ocean again; and not more by virtue of abiding and beneficent law, than do the forms of lichen, of moss, of fungus and fern deposit their spores, and plant their beauteous shapes upon the hideous wall or the unsightly house-top. This harmonizing power, this decorative genius of atom and molecule, is a thing that the atheist and evolutionist will do well to ponder carefully. The development of the individual species is one thing, its adaptation and adjustment to each and all that surround it is quite another. What can be more delightful to contemplate in Nature than the resurrection of beauty from the ashes of the hideous? what more pleasing to reflect upon than the enduring power of her beneficent touch, which no lapse of ages can destroy?

In the rugged and stony soil of the mountains to erect a grave by the casting of stones is a less arduous process than to excavate it with pick and mattock. And the mountain wolves which must have been common in the days of Dunmail would more readily unearth the gravel than burrow through the blocks of the cairn. Barrows, however, in the lower ground must always have exceeded cairns in number. Not a mile from the spot where I wrote these words, there rises from a level meadow the rounded heap which passes in tradition for the 'Grave of Ella.' The ancient barrow was a kind of natural crematorium, more perfect, probably by virtue of its greater exposure to the elements, than is the modern grave. And the cairn, too, upon the mountain would be more perfect still by the ceaseless permeations of the rain storm and the snow. To search for the remains of mortality in a cairn would be like looking for water in a sieve.

The burial of a *Sow* on a dark stormy night, the picks resounding among the hills and the work going on 'by the lantern dimly burning,' was a sight which the writer once witnessed (at a distance) with melancholy interest.

What a saga might thereon have been indited. How earnest were the efforts to save the prolific mother as she lay and gasped out her poor life, and how assiduously and tenderly were her unconscious sucklings cared for by the farmer's family! How they screamed for the comforting bottle, and how plump and joyful they grew up to maturity!

One of the most trying features in the life of farmers holding stock is the sudden illness of an animal in the night-time, with no farrier at hand. On such occasions the solemn consultations, the long night-watchings, the concocting of hot gruel, and general solicitude for the dumb patient, might often put to shame the languid efforts of those in charge of poor humanity.

The life of a fellside farmer is not *all* poetry. Look at the passionate shepherd's song :

> 'Come, live with me and be my love,
>   And we will all the pleasures prove
>   That hills and valleys, dale and field,
>   And all the craggy mountains yield.
>
> 'There will we sit upon the rocks,
>   And see the shepherds feed their flocks
>   By shallow rivers, to whose fall
>   Melodious birds sing madrigaL'

Compare this with the scene of operations on a dark February morning, about five or six o'clock. Out go the sturdy sons of the soil, in the dark, with clogs clattering upon the cobbles, lantern in hand, to look after sick sow, asthmatic calf, wandering sheep, and others of their numerous tribe, and that, too, after watching, perhaps, half the night, and *minus breakfast*. The song they sing within them is but little after Marlowe, and may be supposed to run somewhat in this style :

> 'Oh ! it's up in the morning at five,
>   And out in the teeth of the blast ;
> When the wind on the fell's fit to flay you alive,
>   And the rain might be raining its last !
>
> 'And it's toil, toil, toil,
>   And trudge, trudge, trudge ;
> For small is the fruit of a shepherd's moil,
>   When the elements bear him a grudge.'

S. B.

A townsman, indeed, would scarcely credit the narrative of work performed by some of the sheep-farmers, and it is marvellous how few accidents occur even when snow lies thick upon the hills; but they have narrow escapes at times in rescuing sheep on the fells.

Local family names do not present much that is peculiar to this district, being such as are to be found in other parts of Cumberland. Some of the older families of the last generation have departed, having sold their estates to the Manchester Corporation. The Corporation own the lake and the land contiguous to it.

The chief names now occurring are the following: Hinde, Thwaite, Cole, Walker, Birkett (in the female line), Hawkrigg, Thompson, Bell, and, till recently, Gilbanks.

Cole, we may note, represents the older form of 'coal,' and doubtless the older form of the article also—not 'sea-coal,' but timber. In the old registers 'colliers,' or 'collyers,' were those who attended to the supply of wood fuel for the bloomeries, blomaries, or bloom-smithies, which at one period were suppressed in some districts by royal mandate, on account of their consumption of the wood needful for other uses.

Ashburner, a name very local in the Furness district of Lancashire, refers to the same work, to wit, that of these smelting places which were scattered all

about the country when the great iron-works were unknown.

Thwaite, a place as well as a personal name, abounds
in Cumberland, Westmorland, North Lancashire,
and Yorkshire, with and without a vast variety of
prefixes. The thwaite, or 'clearing' of the cross,
fragrant with memories of St. Kentigern and St.
Hubert, is the ancient site upon which arose the now
venerable church of Crosthwaite, to which that of
Wythburn was long a chapel of ease, and to which it
still pays tithe. Thwaite is by natives usually pronounced T'wait.

The names of Hinde, Walker, Thompson, and Bell
present nothing etymologically that is peculiar to the
district, and are English rather than Cumbrian.

Birkett and Hawkrigg are suggestive.

Birkett in other places assumes a variety of forms,
and is very frequent all round Keswick, the members
of this family forming quite a clan, of which many
members have been highly respected in this district
for generations.

The object-names Hawk and Rigg, combined in
Hawkrigg, remind us of an ornithological feature of
the 'ridges' and rocks in the vicinity of Wythburn,
viz., the abundance, greater in former days than now,
of the falcon tribe. Proportionate to this abundance
is the absence of skylarks in the lower ground, due
apparently to the ease with which their enemy, dashing
from his home upon the cliff, might secure them in

mid-air while soaring from the valley beneath. This name of Hawkrigg, a highly-respected name in Wythburn and St. John's in the Vale, is singularly appropriate to the part of Wythburn about the City and Westhead.

The City,* as has been suggested by one who is no mean scholar, is neither more nor less than a corruption of 'Sitting,' that is, the place of session of the early judges, met to adjudicate in criminal cases. We can then picture the white-bearded patriarchs seated in solemn conclave upon the semicircle of boulders facing the central rock, and, after the giving of sentence, sternly watching the miserable captive led away to be decapitated on that very rock, before the assembled witnesses.

The name of Walker, as Canon C. W. Bardsley tells us, signifies, not a person of great walking power, but a fuller. He quotes a statute of Elizabeth, which includes a 'woollen weaver, cloth-fuller, otherwise called tucker or *walker.*'

* This word 'City' is also the traditional name of a hamlet adjoining the now busy town of St. Helens in Lancashire.

CHAPTER XII.

NORSE ORIGIN OF DIALECT—FANNY GRAHAM—THE
POSTMAN AND THE CALF—MID-COUNTY DIALECT
BALLAD.

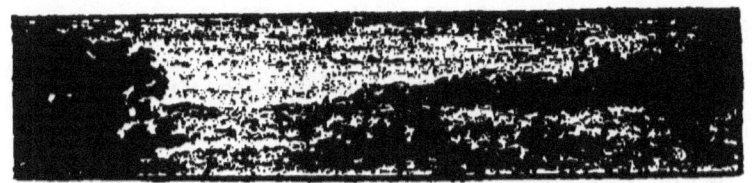

XII.

SPEAKING of the settlement of Adam of Leece at Ulverston, Canon Bardsley remarks: 'Adam of Leece settles in Ulverston as a good centre of industry, but Roger of Ulverston does not settle in Leece. Hence Leece in our registers but not Ulverston.* These local terms,' he adds, 'single or compound, are reminders of a far more distant immigration, that of the Norseman. In *beck*, and *gill*, and *tarn*, and *dale*, and *force* or *foss*, and *fell*, and *scale*, and *holme*, and *thwaite*, and *mire*, we see affixes or suffixes which tell us the particular race that ran their adventurous ships upon the perilous coasts of Cumberland and Furness. It was a Norwegian rather than a Danish raid.' In other ways, too, this author notes that the dialect of Furness indicates 'clear traces of this dim and far-off invasion.'

The above remarks apply very generally to Wythburn and other districts in Cumberland.

* 'Chronicles of the Town and Church of Ulverston.'

To those who are not familiar with this northern dialect, the following specimens* of the style and humour of the people may not be devoid of interest.

The hardiness of some of the poor people is phenomenal.

Fanny Graham, when ninety-three years of age, walked one morning from Lazonby to Plumpton, between four and five miles.

The Rev. Mr. Harrison, meeting her, said :

'I wonder, Fanny, you don't walk with a stick.'

'Shaff o' ye,' says Fanny, 'it's nought but pride o' ye. I rackon nought of fwok walking wid a stick till they're up in years a bit.'

A neighbouring old woman called to see her during the keen cold of the early part of January, 1871, when Fanny was about ninety-seven and still fresh. Bewailing their hard fate, she said :

'Oh dear, Fanny! this hard weather 'ill finish beàth thee and me, I think.'

'Humph!' says Fanny, 'a likely story, indeed! Thou mun speak for thysel'; I'll git through't, I'll warrant me. Dee, indeed! What's to make us dee, I wonder? We sartenly can stand a bit cold like this!'

A postman in the far west of the county overtook a

* From 'Cumbriana,' by the kind permission of Messrs. Callander and Dixon.

butcher leading a calf by a cord tied round his own waist, and vainly endeavouring to induce the animal to cross a foot-bridge on the path. The butcher requested the postman to stand behind the calf and blow his horn when the calf was got into a favourable position.

When the word was given to 'Blaa, Jimmy, blaa!' a sudden and loud blast was given, and over leapt the calf into a deep moss-pool, dragging the butcher along with it. On recovering his feet, he turned to the astonished postman and roared out :

'Thaaw fooal, thaaw ! That was far oor girt a blaa for a fat cofe.'

As an illustration of the power of the vernacular, the following is significant :

Doctor, to sick child : ' Open your mouth, child, and put out your tongue.'

No response, but·a vacant stare.

' This must be a very stupid child of yours, my good woman.'

' It's ye 'at's stupid. Neabody but a feull wad talk tul a bairn that way. Oppen thy gob, hinny, and put out thy lolly.'

The child was all obedience when addressed in a language it understood.

As a memorandum of the good old times, when people more easily made a living, the following verses illustrate the mid-county dialect (' Cumbriana,' p. 236):

'Fwok tells of oald times—sek good oald times
 They hed when they were o' young,
And niver sek times sen them oald times
 Was read on or heard on or sung.

I' winter time, when t' weather was coald,
 They hardly stirrt out at neuk ;
Bit to fetch in a trugful o' peats 'cross t' foald
 And sledder about and smeuk.

They wad thresh a bit, mebby, and fodder their kye,
 And poo a lock out o' t' hay mew ;
And at neet after milkin', and supper put bye,
 Mak swills, or wad card skin woo.

Or mappen wad beetle a carlin sark,
 On t' beetlin' steann at t' door,
Or plet a few strings o' hemp efter dark,
 Or caper about on t' clay floor.

A carlin sark, new, was rumplement gear,
 To wear next a maisterman's skin ;
So he lent it to t' sarvent to beetle and wear,
 By way of a brekkin in.

T' oald fwok were drist in a duffel blue,
 And t' youngsters in heàmm-spun gray ;
And nowder were often ower cleàn or new—
 Bit darn't frae day to day.

And o' wad hev bracken or strea in their clogs,
 Or stickin' ower t' edge o' their shun,
And wad clammer up t' fell, or striddle through bogs,
 Od, man ! but this was laal fun.'   Etc.

CHAPTER XIII.

MAN AND NATURE—WATERSHED—ANCIENT WOODS—
POET'S WALK—MUTATIONS OF OXYGEN.

XIII.

CONSPICUOUS upon the summit of the ridge of rocks that overhang the farm of Westhead are two stone figures built of small boulders from the fell and styled by the natives, the 'Modest Man' and the 'Modest Woman.' It is pretty well-known that these were erected by some young men, residing at one of the farms within recent years. It is astonishing how long such structures will endure in so exposed a situation. This remark applies also to the walls, devoid of mortar, that mark the higher ground. The latter are, however, subject to continual rebuilding of the upper portion, each farmer being responsible for his own. The work of man, even here, has had a considerable effect in modifying nature. Allusion has been made to the 'bloom-smithies' and their influence first in denuding and afterwards covering the country again with plantations. So thick were the woods in former days between the Valley of Wythburn and the town of Keswick, that it is said to have been a remark of the natives, that a squirrel

might have travelled from Wythburn Church to
Keswick without ever touching ground. Whether the
Manchester Corporation will think it desirable to
plant afresh upon the hill-sides, now bare enough in
most parts, remains to be seen. The ground is,
first and foremost, a watershed for the Lake of
Thirlmere—now, or soon to be, a reservoir for the
city of Manchester. Will the extension of the woods
increase the quantity or improve the quality of the
water? Experts must decide. But one thing seems
plain enough, that woods upon a hill-side must
tend to moderate its descent. It is, I believe, allowed
that where a large tract of land with heavy rain-fall has
been much stripped, the torrents have become the
more unmanageable, and floods more dangerous and
excessive. And it will not be disputed that woods
have a tendency to attract vapour and to distil the
freight of the passing clouds.

It would seem, therefore, that with regard to
the descent of water, woods are in two respects
desirable, and the question of their influence on
quality remains. This is partly solved already. For
if the lake of Thirlmere, with the mass of timber
now around it, yields water as pure as it undoubtedly
is, it seems unreasonable to imagine that a judicious
planting of the hill slopes again would in any appreci-
able degree deteriorate it. Whether these considera-
tions will weigh with the Manchester Corporation
time alone can show; but that the beauty of the

district would be enhanced by an extension of the woods few, I think, will deny.

The new road to the west of Thirlmere, opening out as it does such lovely views to the tourist, will largely compensate for other changes that many might be disposed to deplore. The walk over the hills to Watendlath will by it be made shorter, for intending pedestrians can then alight from their carriages and ascend at Armboth. This was a walk that the poets delighted in; Wordsworth, Coleridge, De Quincey, Arnold, Rossetti, Faber, must have been in their element here. The solemn and the beautiful, the impressive and the tender, things vast and delicate and mysterious, the romance of history and the inner shrine of Nature's sanctuary, the borderland of the visible and the invisible, ever changing and ever fresh, are here. Here, indeed, is the Kingdom of Oxygen.

Looking at the little forces which man exerts upon the earth, how utterly futile they seem when contrasted with the silent, continuous action of those in Nature's machinery. The marvellous magic-working substance we call Oxygen—how various, how immense are its operations! Now it breaks to powder and brings to dust the hardest stone or the toughest metal; again, it paints with beauty and kindles with fresh bloom the rosy face of a child; now it builds up a crystal or a flower, and again, it tears to pieces their shattered remains; now it fills the air with freshness and life; again, it gives fierce destructive power to the conflagration that lays a city in ashes. Ever active, ever changing its form, its operations, in quantity, energy and variety, exceeds the dreams of human arithmetic. Inscribed on every page of Nature's book, he that runs may read:

'Ars-celare artem.'

And here is art that *never wearies.*

Ten thousand times ten thousand metamorphoses, continued unintermittingly from that day 'when the morning stars sang together and all the sons of God shouted for joy' to the present time, have not sufficient to destroy the character of that wonder-working gas—or fairy—which we term Oxygen. Endless must have been the migrations, inconceivable the work of almost every particle of it that enters into the outer crust of the earth, yet it is still young and active, or man's days would soon be ended. Whence comes this immense, unchangeable and sublime vitality? Echo, like the materialist of to-day, answers —where? But the poet replies: By the law of Duty, by the fiat of The Eternal:

'Flowers laugh before Thee in their beds,
  And fragrance in Thy footing treads;
  Thou dost preserve the stars from wrong,
  And the most ancient heavens by Thee are fresh and
    strong.'

CHAPTER XIV

XIV.

'Neither is there any rock like our God.'—1 SAM. ii. 2.

LONG ages ago, in that remote and forgotten past when man, defenceless and illiterate, fled from his stronger fellows to the fastnesses of the mountains, he found in their solemn and majestic forms a fascination full of mystery and awe.

The faculty of worship and the sense of unseen existences readily associated themselves with the most striking of Nature's forms, and the traditional vestiges of a Divine revelation gave solemnity and interest to the customs of his tribes. Thus the mountains have, from the earliest dawn of history, been regarded as the embodiment of spiritual powers, as the type of enduring strength, of purity, and of truth. The living streams, that descend from their cloud-capped summits to revive the thirsty cattle that wander over their verdant sides, have rightly been regarded as fitting symbols of that spirit-life and refreshment whose source is eternal in the heavens; and the peaceful lakes that slumber at their feet, and mirror the beauty of the sky, have justly been taken—at least by the Christian—as picturing the fulness of Divine love; the inexhaustible fountain of cleansing and of peace.

How inestimable are the blessings of the rain and dew distilled from the treasures of the air by the attractive force of the everlasting hills! They descend to water the thirsty plain and restore the fainting myriads of the close-pent city, they facilitate by the force of their streams the operations of industry; they form the most delightful means of transit; they are the avenues to a thousand varieties of human enjoyment. How sublime, too, are the thoughts suggested by the mountain torrent, and the living waters that owe their birth to its moss-crowned crags!

'There is a river, the streams whereof shall make glad the city of God, the holy place of the tabernacles of the Most High.'

'I will look unto the hills, from whence cometh my help.'

'And he arose and did eat and drink, and went in the strength of that meat forty days and forty nights unto Horeb the Mount of God.'

'The strength of the hills is His also.'

'Who shall ascend into the hill of the Lord?'

Thus nobly does the grand old language of the Hebrew poets bring before us both the beauties of Nature's face and the glorious truths which they symbolize in the spirit world the Divine handiwork and its lessons; and chief among these, the things that they reveal concerning the Lord Himself. 'Acquaint thyself with Him and be at peace, so shall good come unto thee;' thus wrote the poet-dramatist of Nature in the early dawn of the Church's history; so taught the Lord Jesus, Himself the true and living way to the Father. 'This is life eternal that they might know Thee, the only true God, and Jesus Christ whom Thou hast sent.'

When Hannah uttered in her sublime song of praise the striking words of the text, a great crisis was approaching in the history of the chosen people. It was near at hand. Wickedness had found its way into high places, and crimes of the deepest dye stained the characters of those who should have been the leaders of the nation. The measure of their iniquity was now full, and the axe was laid to the root of the tree. The Lord arose 'as a man of war' to avenge His people.

Therefore the song of this mother in Israel sounds a clear note of triumph: it is the triumph of right over wrong, of holiness over corruption, of humble and neglected worth over the vain and short-lived boasting of the tyrant of this world: it is the triumph of the Lord Himself over His adversaries. Such a song, too, was that of Mary, when, in the fulness of time the Lord appeared to redeem His people; a song perhaps not mightier than this of Hannah, but relative to a grander theme. 'He hath showed strength with

His arm; He hath scattered the proud in the imagination of their hearts.'

We observe that in the songs of Hannah, and of Miriam, of Deborah and Mary, in the utterance of power from the mouth of a woman, there appears the evidence of that wisdom of God which chooseth the weak things of the world to confound the strong. May we not add too, that this wisdom, exercised in the government of the world is in perfect agreement with the plan observed in Nature, where results of the first importance are effected by a mechanism so simple as almost to elude observation? In all these things we own the master touch of the Supreme Architect as well as the glory of His work, whether it be in nature or in human history; and we realize the force of the patriarch's question, 'Canst thou by searching find out God?' and that word, too, of the Psalmist, 'Thou art a God that hidest Thyself.'

And ought we not also to realize the force of that grand lesson shown in the history of His Church, a lesson that has so tried the patience of His people to learn, viz., that 'Though clouds and darkness are about Him, righteousness and judgment are the habitation of His seat?'

Yes: 'There is no rock like our God,' none like Him for mystery and for majesty; for perfection in plan, and for excellence in working; it is He alone who, both in nature and in history, bringeth mighty things to pass.

Would that we all could realize in our own hearts the grand sustaining power of this blessed and eternal truth—that God is infallibly and absolutely just!

In the contemplation of Nature under the solemn shade and mighty presence of Helvellyn, a hill so well-known to traveller and poet, we are led first to consider the rock, as forming the mountain that adorns the landscape.

And therefore I call attention to its solemn mysterious grandeur; its vastness, its impressive power and mysterious suggestiveness.

These characteristics belong more or less to every mountain, from the glorious peaks of the Andes and Himalayas to the fern-clad slopes and mossy peaks of our own varied Lake district. The sublime aspects of every mountain range, the world over, speak to the human race like an abiding voice with an ever-enduring lesson, to tell the vastness of the Divine plan, the perfection of the Divine architecture and the insignificance of man. And who will deny that these are lessons which it is very wholesome for us all to learn? Amid the harassing cares, the feverish competition, the losses and the sorrows of an ever-changing life, to be alone for a time amid the pure, refreshing and hope-inspiring influences of mountain and vale, of moor and torrent, is like a draught of nectar to the thirsty soul.

And the sense of a perennial constancy that breathes through the wilder scenes of Nature's wondrous archi-

tecture is a mighty power to soothe and to heal. It
falls upon the spirit with the sweet calm and solemn
music of an enduring sabbath. Amid these peaceful
scenes the vision and the hope of those pictured
glories of seer and prophet seem unfolded to our view,
for the grandest strains of prophet and psalmist are
always in harmony with the voice of the everlasting
hills. And, both from our own meditations and from
the inspired pages, one grand lesson should come
home to every thoughtful mind. It is set forth in the
sublime words of Milton :

> ‘ These are Thy glorious works, Parent of good,
> Almighty ! Thine this universal frame
> Thus wondrous fair ; Thyself how wondrous then,
> Unspeakable, that sit'st above these heavens
> To us invisible, or dimly seen
> In these Thy lowest works ; yet these declare
> Thy goodness beyond thought and power Divine.’

And if we admit with our greatest philosopher
that it is better to believe all the fables of the
Koran, than that the universal frame of nature is
without a controlling mind, we must also acknow-
ledge that the Divine plan and purpose have con-
trolled it from the beginning and will control it to the
end. Some of you will have read of a great man who
lay fretting upon his bed, as to what would happen
when he was taken from the world—‘ Sir,’ said his
servant, ‘ don't you think that God managed this world
before you were brought into it ?’ ‘ True, indeed,’

said the master. 'Then, sir,' replied the servant, 'cannot you trust Him to manage it when you are gone?'

The kindly reproof was not without effect; it calmed the troubled spirit. And, indeed, if we could but regard aright this mighty spectacle of Divine government in the world about us we should gladly perceive the force of our Blessed Lord's utterance concerning one of His miracles—' My Father worketh *hitherto* and I work.'

Throughout the long continued conflict waged in both the realms of nature—animate and inanimate— to effect, in the one the balance of opposing forces, in the other the preservation of life, a mighty arm has held the reins and directed the advance of those mysterious wheels which the prophet beheld—full of eyes, animated by living spirits, and terrible in their vast circumference.

Balance and mutual attraction amid the mighty orbs that circle through the fields of space; balance in the winds that course about our planet and in the clouds that water the thirsty soil; balance in the tides that roll their ceaseless course from shore to shore; balance throughout the realms of the animated world, and a limit assigned to the increase and the habitation of every creature; balance of every constant exactness in the very affinities of the atoms and elements that compose the soil; and the hand that poises the scales through all this unimaginable diversity of government more unshaken in strength than the foundation of Himalayas or of Andes, and more pure in equity than the virgin snows that robe their summits.

Such is the spectacle that the broader aspects of nature present to the devout believer. And when we turn to look more closely at the structure of this wondrous world, we find the various parts that compose it no less fertile in their teaching. The spiritual lessons, which nature seems to retain for the thoughtful, as the philosophers of old preserved their choicest enigmas for the true votaries of their science, will often be found most striking. The value of such works as 'Bible Teachings in Nature,' 'Natural Law in the Spiritual World,' is great, not merely as affording intellectual refreshment together with striking illustrations of spiritual truth, but specially as presenting to us a clearer view of the grand unity of Nature and a suggestive reminder that her teaching is co-extensive with her dominion. Bird and beast, insect and flower, earth, sea and sky, are ever opening before us a volume of lessons that expand more and more as the faculty of observation is developed within us.

Look at the multitude of tiny creatures—fern and flower and moss in all their varieties—that find a habitation upon our lonely hill-sides. Who would have imagined that the 'gentle rain from heaven' and those minute forms of life could modify, as they have done, the hard volcanic rock that surrounds us here? Yet by such tiny creatures is the soil produced, and the very character of our scenery determined. How true it is that in the natural world, as in the spiritual, the work accomplished by the weak things in the end surpasses that of the strong. And in both worlds, we shall do well to notice the evidences of His hand who is not dependent on instruments, but *creates* them, to effect His purposes, for history as well as the life of individuals abounds with illustrations of the truth that 'great events from trifling causes spring.' And we may ask, how can an event be really trifling if great ones depend upon it? And again—who but He, who holds in His hand both great and small, can control the chain of circumstances?

The mighty rock and the tender little plants that cluster upon it are inseparably connected. They clothe its rugged sides with a garment of beauty, they mould its outline, and add expression to the landscape. The effect of their work continued through the ages is incalculable. Let us read in this parable of nature these comforting truths—first, that the lives and the prayers of the little ones are effectual with God; second, that little deeds in the aggregate lead to grand results; third, that His helpless and innocent ones are specially dear to the Great Father of all.

A simple-minded and faithful woman once sympathized with a great missionary, and toiled with diligence to advance his work for Christ. 'Greet Mary, who bestowed much labour upon us,' writes St. Paul to the Romans. Those nameless little acts of sympathetic care and industry have gained for Mary an imperishable name, a name fragrant with holy love, a name which is inscribed in the Book of God for ever.

Thus in nature and in the pages of Holy Scripture we may see, if we will, touches of infinite tenderness —illustrations of the truth that He who hath His dwelling so high—the High and Holy One that inhabiteth eternity—can condescend to dwell with him that is of a lowly and contrite spirit, and can say of all His innocent children, 'Suffer them to come unto Me.'

And now we turn to consider that eternal Rock from whence flows the stream of our salvation, that stream of which it was written by the Psalmist, 'There is a river the streams whereof shall make glad the City of God. The holy place of the tabernacles of the Most High.' That Rock, once smitten for us, hath sent forth abundantly the healing waters through the wilderness of this perishing world. Will ye come to these mighty waters and wash and be healed, or will ye turn to the profitless Abana and Pharpar of the City of Destruction?

> 'Rock of Ages, cleft for me,
> Let me hide myself in Thee !
> Let the water and the blood
> From Thy riven side which flowed
> Be of sin the double cure :
> Cleanse me from its guilt and power !'

So let us learn an abiding lesson from :—1, the loftiness and purity ; 2, the strength and endurance ;

3, the life-giving streams of the 'Mountains of God.' Truly, if any object in nature can be worthy of the grand old Hebrew phrase, it is a glorious mountain with its peaks encircled by the mystery of cloudland, with its verdant pastures and bubbling brooks. We gaze across the valley when the cloud-procession is moving from pass to pass in its majestic array, and the crests beyond lift up their snowy summits into the glorious serenity of the unsullied sky. They look down as it were with compassion upon the troubles and turmoil of this mortal strife. They speak to us and tell us to look to Him who sitteth above the heavens. 'Be ye holy,' they say, 'for the Lord your God is holy.' 'As the heavens are higher than the earth, so are My ways higher than your ways, and My thoughts than your thoughts.' There is no rock so high as our God, in purity, in holiness and love. Again, the mountains are strong and endure. They resist the batteries of the storm from age to age, their inaccessible strongholds become the refuge of the outcast and the vanquished, and when nations have flourished and passed away and their very names are forgotten, these silent preachers endure. They point to heaven to tell us that our home is *there* and not upon earth; with solemn and majestic voice they rebuke the mad passions, the insane cupidity, the debasing frivolities of men; but their grandest lesson, their peculiar voice consists in this, that they are the 'Mountains of God.' They are His, and of Him they speak.

Compared with the greatest works of man, the mountains are indeed everlasting; but moss and raindrop,
snow and storm are surely though slowly, bringing
down their pride to the valleys beneath; it is the
Lord alone who endureth throughout all generations,
and who changeth the face of nature as a garment.
It is the Lord only who is a sure refuge for the
oppressed from all their enemies, their castle to which
they may continually resort. Pure, indeed, and refreshing are the streams that well forth from the solitudes
of the mighty hills, but those who drink of their
waters shall thirst again. The Lord alone is that
Eternal Rock from which floweth the water of life,
the perennial stream of which, if a man drink, he shal
live for ever.

May it be the blessed privilege of all who read
these words to draw from the wells of salvation that
spiritual life which shall bear fruit for ever in the
paradise of God !

> ' I heard the voice of Jesus say,
>   " Behold I freely give
> The living water, thirsty one,
>   Stoop down, and drink, and live :"
> I came to Jesus, and I drank
>   Of that life-giving stream ;
> My thirst was quenched, my soul revived,
>   And now I live in Him.'

THE END.

Elliot Stock, 62, Paternoster Row, London, E.C.